LOTTERY BOY

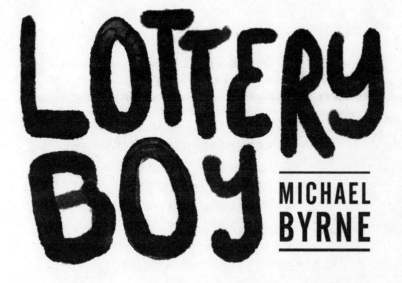

LOTTERY BOY

MICHAEL BYRNE

WALKER
BOOKS

First published 2015 by Walker Books Ltd
87 Vauxhall Walk, London SE11 5HJ

2 4 6 8 10 9 7 5 3 1

Text © 2015 Michael Byrne
Cover images: Boy running © Red Edge / Anna Baria;
Chasing men © Sean Murphy / Getty Images, Inc

This book has been typeset in Minion Pro

Printed and bound in Great Britain by Clays Ltd, St Ives plc

British Library Cataloguing in Publication Data:
a catalogue record for this book is available from the British Library

ISBN 978-1-4063-5829-2

www.walker.co.uk

For my daughter, Eve

"Dreams are true while they last,
and do we not live in dreams?"
Alfred, Lord Tennyson

05 **05** **19**
DAYS HOURS MINUTES

Bully squinted up at one of the faces of the big, big clock across the river. Both hands were going past the six and it was time for Jack's tea. He pulled the can and metal spoon out of his long coat pocket.

"Here you go… Here's your tea, mate," he said, making a big fuss of spooning it out, because there was only jelly in the bottom. Jack sucked it down without chewing.

Jack was a bull terrier, a Staffy cross, but crossed with what Bully didn't know for sure, no one did. That other half was all mixed up bits of other dogs. Her short wiry fur was dark brown around the neck and streaked white and grey everywhere else, making her look like an old dog at the end of her days. And she had a Monkey Dog tail, and a wide back with legs that were jacked up at the rear and bowed at the front, so that when she sat up she looked like she *really* wanted to hug you. Her head, though, had little fangy teeth inside so that you didn't *really* want to hug her.

When Bully had left the flat in the winter, Jack had come with him. It was the summer now and though she was getting on for two years old and filling out, she was still a funny-looking dog. Not a good dog for begging, but to Bully she wasn't for begging. She was his friend and as good as family.

"Come on, mate ... come on..." Bully pleaded because Jack was still looking at him and now there was nothing much left in the can. Still, he had another scrape round. Then without thinking he slid the spoon into his own mouth. It came on him like that when he was hungry – all of a sudden, catching him out, making him do strange things – like he couldn't control it, like *he* was the animal.

Bully spat it out. The jelly didn't taste so bad but it was the feel of it he didn't like, cold and slimy in the back of his mouth. He rinsed his cheeks out with water and then from habit, to calm himself down, he read the ingredients listed on the back of the tin because he liked things that just told you what they were and didn't try telling you anything else.

Water 65%

Protein 20%

Fat 12%...

He got down to the last ingredient, the only one that he didn't like seeing there: *Ash 3%*. And he thought of all the zombies in the factories flicking their fags and topping up the cans. And the other kinds of ash they used, maybe, if they ran out of smokes. But at least they were honest enough to put it on the back of the tin.

He went to lob the can into the river but changed his mind when he saw the picture of the dog. It was a Jack Russell. And he liked Jack Russell terriers – a bit too little maybe, a bit too yappy – but what he *really* loved was seeing Jack's name printed out on the label. It made *his* dog sound important and official. Though Jack wasn't technically a dog. *She* was really a girl dog – what they called in the dog magazines a *bitch*. And when he'd found her all that long time ago, last summer, and brought her back to the flat, and Phil had pointed out she was a *girl*, he'd named her *Jacky* straight away before his mum got back from the hospital. Bully, though, hadn't called her that since he'd left the flat. He'd lost the *y*, so she was just Jack now.

He put the empty can in his coat pocket and wandered back along the river towards the big white Eye that always looked broken to him – the way the wheel went round without moving, like the zombies stuck up there were waving for help. Jack followed along next to him, every so often nosing his ankles but never getting under his feet. Bully had trained her pretty well before they left the flat. He'd spent weeks just teaching her to *stay*, giving her Haribo and Skittles whenever she did it right. They called that *rewarding good behaviour* in the magazines.

Bully stopped when he got to the skateboard park, sucked in by the clatter of the boards and the laughter. He didn't think much of the place though. There weren't any big ramps or jumps, just little concrete ones no bigger than some of the kerbs and speed bumps on his old estate. He didn't even think it was a *real* skateboard park, the way it was squeezed underneath the big fat grey building above. And it reminded Bully of the block of flats where he used to live, the basement underneath where the rubbish chutes fed down to the bins.

He still didn't know any of the boys who did tricks. He just came here to watch them laughing and talking and falling off, and then blaming their skateboards for everything. One day he'd rock up with a board that you couldn't blame anything on, with silver and gold trucks and the best decals … and it would be just the best one. He wasn't sure when that day would be but it would definitely be a day.

"Look at 'im," he said, pointing one of them out to Jack. "Shit, in 'e?" Secretly, though, he hoped that if he just stood there and stared long enough, one day one of them might let him have a go. So far all they'd done was call him a *germ* and tell him to eff off. He didn't know exactly what a germ was in skater speak but he knew it was something little and dirty and *bad*. Though to be fair, when he was here with Chris and Tiggs, Chris had called them a lot worse names and thrown that bottle so that it smashed right in the middle of where they did their crappy tricks.

That didn't happen usually. Usually they just lobbed their empties off the footbridge to watch them float back underneath. Chris and Tiggs were his mates. They said things, making him laugh, going on about girls who were *pigeon* and *breezy*, messing about along the river. Chris sometimes tied a red bit of rag round his head and Tiggs *always* had his big extra ears somewhere on his head, listening to his *sick tunes*. They were both older than him. And they had been all over the place, all over London, even up to Brent Cross shopping centre.

He watched the skaters for a bit longer until a short little boy, shorter than him, did a *really* crappy trick and fell right off onto the concrete slabs, rolling over and skinning his elbow and rubbing it like that would make the skin come back. Bully started fake laughing. He knew they wouldn't do anything because he had Jack with him but he didn't want the Feds getting wind, so they left and carried on walking towards the Eye.

At the footbridge he stared at the beggar man on the bottom step. He wasn't doing it right. Usually, if you were begging you sat at the top where the zombies stopped to catch their breath. The man didn't look too good either, shivering in the sun, wouldn't be making much with his head down, mumbling to himself like that but not saying a word. He didn't even have a sign. You had to have a sign if you weren't going to ask, otherwise how was anyone to know?

Bully went round the beggar man and climbed halfway up the steps to the footbridge. He stopped and looked back along the river to see if there was anything worth fishing for. The sun was still warm on the backs of his legs and a long way from touching the water, not the best time of day for fishing. There were still too many zombies about, not looking right or left, but leaving town as fast as they could. And in the morning, coming back just as quick. He squinted a little more to sharpen up his eyesight. Everything wriggled in front of him if he didn't squint. He was supposed to wear glasses for seeing things a long way away but he'd left the flat without them, so he just squashed his eyes and squinted instead.

He made out a couple of maybes leaning over the railings, looking at the river: a tall girl in shorts and tights with an ice cream, her boyfriend smaller than her, joking about, pretending to rob it off her. Bully left them alone though. Girls didn't like dogs but old ladies did. And there was one! With a nice big handbag on her arm large enough to fit Jack in, staring at buildings across the river like she'd never seen a window before. He went down the steps on tiptoe quick as he could, nearly tripping over the guy still shivering away on the bottom step, and came up on her blind side just as she was starting to move on.

He matched his pace with hers.

"I'm trying to get back to me mum's, but I'm short 59 p…"

"Oh, right," she said, but stepping back like it wasn't right.

"I want to go home but I'm short," he said, a little faster in case she got away.

Bully liked to make it sound as if he needed the money for something else, that he wasn't just begging, otherwise they started asking you all sort of questions about what you were doing and why weren't you at school. He'd learnt that.

"So can you do us a favour?"

She looked like she was ready to turn her head away, knock him back with a "no, thank you", but then she looked down and saw Jack there.

"Oh… Is that your dog?"

"Yeah."

"He's a good dog, isn't he?" she said.

"Yeah…" He nodded but only to himself and tried not

to pull a face. Of course she was. Bully had taught her to be a good dog and to do as she was told because that's what you did. You didn't treat a dog *like* a dog and shout and hit it. What you did was, you trained a dog up so that it *obeyed* you, and then you had a friend for life.

"Have you got 59 pence then or what? I wouldn't ask normally." He always said this, though he never really thought about what *was* normal any more. Once, an old lady, even older than this one, with a hat and a stick and off her head, had taken him to a café and bought him a fry-up and they'd sat there in the warm for an hour, her telling him things about when she was a girl and lived in the countryside and had her own horse and a springer spaniel, but that wasn't *normal*. Sometimes he got a whole quid out of it, often just pennies and shrapnel. Once, he got exactly what he asked for to the penny, a young guy counting it out in front of his mates for a laugh and that had really wound him up.

"How old are you?"

"Sixteen."

"You sure?"

"I'm small for me age, innit," he said.

She made those tiny eyes that grown-ups did when they were having a good look at you from inside their head. He reckoned he could just about pass for sixteen with his hat on. It was a sauce-brown beanie hat with black spots. And it was his. He'd remembered to take it from the flat when he left in the winter. He didn't need to wear it to keep warm any more but it hid his face from the cameras in the station and made him taller. He fiddled with it, pulled it up to a point so that in the summer sun he looked like one of Santa's little helpers who was way too big for next Christmas.

He was twelve but getting closer to thirteen now so that he could count out the months in between just using one hand. When he was at little school, he'd been the tallest boy in the year, taller even than the tallest *girl*. And already he was 167 centimetres and a bit. He had a tape measure in one of his pockets that he'd nicked out the back of a builder's van and in old-fashioned height that was nearly exactly five foot six. And that was bigger than some grown-up men, and as big as some *Feds*. His mum had been tall but, thinking about it, that was because a lot of the time he'd been small. And she'd worn heels. Platform one and platform two she used to call them. Maybe his dad was tall. Maybe his dad could reach up and touch the concrete ceiling at the skateboard park. Anyway, whatever his dad was, he was definitely going to get taller. That was his breed. He'd decided this, because as soon as he was tall enough, he was going to rob a bank or get a job or something and save up and get a proper place with a toilet and a bed and a TV.

He tuned back in. She was still sizing him up.

"Sixteen … are you *really*?"

"Yeah, I had cancer when I was little and that shrunk me up a lot," he said all matter of fact, because cancer did that to you. His mum, after all the hospitals, had never worn heels again.

"Oh, love. You poor love. You go and get home… Look,

get yourself a good meal with this and don't go spending it on anything else, will you?" she said, looking at him now with bigger eyes. Bully didn't like being talked to like that. He could spend it on what he liked if she gave it to him, but his face lit up when he heard the crackle of a note coming out of her purse.

When he saw the colour he couldn't believe it. A bluey! Jack could have tins for a couple of weeks off this, the kind she liked with her name on and only *3% ash*. And he fancied an ice cream and chips for himself and a proper *cold* can of Coke from a shop. He hadn't had a proper can in weeks. Bare expensive in London, a can of Coke was. A total rip-off. That was the first thing that had really shocked him when he got here on the train: the price of a can of Coke.

"There," she said. "You get home soon." She smiled to herself as if she was the one getting the money and walked off towards one of the eating places on the river.

"Cheers, yeah. God bless ya," he said after her. He thought that sounded good. It was what the Daveys said: the old shufflers on the streets with spiders up their noses and kicked-about carpet faces. He'd called them that after one of them had told him his name was Dave. He'd asked for a lend of Bully's mobile and Bully had run away and steered clear of all of them after that.

Jack growled, her quiet warning one, under the radar, just for Bully. He looked up, the queen still smiling at him from off the twenty-pound note. But he lost his smile when he saw who it was, and the dog he had with him. Bully told himself he mustn't run – worse for him later if he did because there was Janks with his eyes shaded out and his lizard grin that said: I know *you*.

Janks robbed beggars all over London town. *Taxing* he called it. He didn't even need the money, just got a kick out of it, that's what they said. They said he'd come down from *up north* and made his money dogfighting and breeding all sorts of illegals, and *the rest* they said. You never usually caught him out and about in the daytime with one of his illegals. Too many Feds. But once in a while, doing his rounds, he liked to chance it, showing off one of his pure-bred pit bulls.

Nasty animals. There were a few breeds Bully wasn't keen on but the only dogs he despised were pit bulls. He didn't like anything about them: the way they strutted about, looking for trouble with their long, shiny, burnt-smooth faces and tiny, beady black eyes. And they had this thing, so they said – everybody said – this click in their jaws like a key in a lock that meant once they bit down and got a hold of you, they never let go. Once on the estate he'd seen an American pit bull turn on the boy walking it and even when his mates had battered it, Old Mac from the newsagent's still had to come out with a crow bar and pry it off.

Janks's pit bull was straining on a long lead, choking itself to get at them. And Jack's growl went up a notch and she started taking little snappy chunks out of the air.

"Stay, mate, stay, stay, stay… Mate!"

Bully's top half swayed and twitched like he was a rat with

its paws stuck in a glue trap, the rest of him still trying to get away. He'd seen them do that – real rats gnaw their own legs off near the bins round the back of the eating places.

He managed to stagger forward just a few steps and kick Jack round behind him because Jack wasn't good at backing down. It was one bit of her training she struggled with. She was fine round people – most people anyway – just some dogs rubbed her up the wrong way.

"You's done well…" Janks said, getting in close so that Bully felt the words on his face. He spoke in a funny way, the words seesawing up and down, the way they did up north. His dog snapped at Jack's face and Jack snapped back and Bully gave her another punt with his toe.

"I taxed you before, didn't I?" said Janks. He pulled Bully's hat off and let it fall. The pit bull instantly went for it – like a nasty game of fetch – and started tearing it apart.

"Grown, 'aven't ya?" he said, ignoring what was going on at his feet.

Bully was close to Janks's height now. When he'd first got to the river in the winter time, a long time ago, this man with the same stickleback bit of hair, the same "nice to know you" smile, had asked for a loan. And when Bully had said no, he'd taken his money anyway and given him a kicking, as if that was paying him back.

Bully had managed to keep out of Janks's way since then.

"You want to mind *that*," he said, nodding down at Jack. "My dog'll rip that thing of yours apart. You don't want to start facing up to me with a dog, boy."

Bully just stood there, too frightened to work out whether to shake his head or nod.

"Calling me out, are you, big man? You giving me the *eyes*?" And Janks jerked Bully's head down in the crook of his arm, pushing his face into his jacket so that Bully could *smell* him – a sort of sharp, sniffy smell like that stuff his mum used to spray round with – and he did his best to breathe through his mouth.

"Stay! Stay, Jack!" Bully's muffled voice just about made it out of the headlock.

"Yeah, that's right. Good *boy*," said Janks, squeezing his neck harder still.

Bully twisted his head to breathe, looked down and saw daylight at Janks's feet. Everyone knew he had a cut-down skewer inside his boot. He'd used it once on a guy, a big fat flubber who wasn't showing him any respect, that's what Chris and Tiggs had told him. And he imagined it happening the way his mum used to do their spuds in the microwave, stabbing them with a fork, quick, before putting them in: *stab, stab, stab.*

"What she give you?"

"Twenty…" Bully said to the feet. He heard a dog yelp.

"Well, lucky for you that's what you owe me."

"*Mate…*" he pleaded.

"Who you talkin' to? I'm not your *mate*."

Bully felt the crook of Janks's arm cut into his windpipe and he started making alphabet sounds like he was a little kid. *K … k … k … a … a … r … r.* His head was thumping because the blood was getting stuck in it but he couldn't say anything, not even sorry, and he felt faint and his legs began to go, making it worse for him.

And then suddenly he could breathe.

"Re-lax … *re-lax*, man…" Janks was patting Bully hard on his back, like he was helping him to cough something up. Bully pulled away, dazed like he'd been trapped underground for a week. He wobbled a bit and saw what Janks was seeing: a couple of fake Feds in high-vis: Community Support Officers standing away by the footbridge with their backs to them, talking to the beggar man.

Bully looked back at Janks who was staring right through him. Then he looked down, saw Jack at his feet, blood dripping off her ear, and his anger roared up quick like a paper fire. And while he waited for it to burn out he thought about what he'd do to Janks one day when he was robbing banks or had a job and was a whole lot bigger than him.

Bully handed the note over and Janks took it without a word. Then he heard a terrible sound: Janks screwing up his twenty quid into a ball, because there was only one thing you did with a ball… And Bully watched Janks walk over to the railings and flick his money into the river.

"Don't keep me waiting next time. *Mate*," he said, smoothing his bit of hair down, a gust of wind blowing it straight back up again. Bully nodded down at the ground, paid his respects and looked away.

When Jack stopped growling, Bully picked his hat up, ripped apart and slick with dog spit, and shoved it in one of his pockets. He checked Jack's ear. It looked worse than it was. Janks's dog had only managed to take a nick out of it. He used the rest of his water to wash the blood off, then gave Jack a squirt of it.

"You got to learn when to back down, mate," he said. Jack didn't seem to be listening, too busy licking Bully's face. "Get off," he said but didn't push her away. He rounded up some of the spit off his cheek and swabbed the wound on her ear because dog spit was good for cuts, as good as medicine (though he had never seen this printed in the magazines).

Eventually he stood up, went and took a long look in the river. He thought maybe he could still see it, a spec of blue, his twenty quid, sailing away under the bridge and out into the sea. The tide was going that way. He caught himself thinking about jumping in after it, though he couldn't swim, not even doggy-paddle. He'd bunked off the school swimming lessons at the leisure centre because he didn't like the noise there in the pool, all the screaming and shouting. He bunked off school too, for the same reason: having to sit still at a desk, questions and answers from thirty other kids all day, right next to his ears. He could just about put up with it when he had his mum to come home to at the end of it all, but after she'd died it was all just empty noise.

He looked back towards the footbridge and one of the fake Feds was looking at him. Bully started walking off, whistled Jack to follow him, getting in step with the zombies until he could cut through between the eating places and make for the station. He thought about taking one of the tunnels to be on the safe side but he didn't like tunnels, even in summer. He didn't like going under the ground if he could help it. Besides, he'd got used to his route: past the fountain that wet the pavement on windy days, across the traffic lights, through the arch, up the steps where the dead train drivers' names were scratched into the walls, and into Waterloo.

Waiting at the traffic lights, he leaned against the railings. He watched a few zombies get ahead of the game, beat the lights, hop and skip between the cars like kids out for the day. He fiddled with one of the red rubber bands he wore on his wrists. He collected them, picked them up off the pavement and at busy times, fired them at the zombies as they raced away. It was a game he played. He'd invented different ways to do it, too – and so far, he'd come up with seven. His favourite, though, was to just ping it off his thumb. And that was what he did … *ping*. A zombie just stepping off the kerb slapped the back of his neck and looked round. Bully gave him the innocent face.

"Big Issue… Help the homeless… Big Issue…" A woman with soft brown eyes was standing a few feet away. She was here most days in the summer now. And he had got used to her.

The green man came and went but Bully wasn't in a rush. He had all day, what was left of it anyway. He did a quick check for Feds, then started patting himself down. He did this ten, twenty times a day depending on the weather. It had become a routine, going through his pockets, making sure he had all his stuff, that he was all there. And it passed the time when he was bored because his coat had a lot of pockets. He'd robbed it from a bag outside a charity shop, leaving his old one there in its place. It was the best coat he'd ever had. *Barbour* it said on the label. It was warm and padded like a blanket inside but with a green and greasy skin to it that stopped the wind and rain like a brick wall. It had been way too big for him in the winter but he was growing into it now and the edge of it left a greasy mark on his jeans just above his knees. The best bit about it was the pockets. He'd never seen a coat like it. It had eleven altogether. The biggest one was like a rubber ring with holes cut in it that ran all the way round the bottom inside. And he'd cut holes in the two for his hands so that he could stash stuff in his jeans without anybody in the shops seeing.

"Big Issue... Help the *hopeless* ... homeless, I mean," the woman said, correcting herself, but no one heard her except Bully. He laughed – not nasty like he had done at the skateboard park because the lady had her long brown hair in a ponytail, like his mum used to wear it when she was working.

He started pulling out the usual bits and pieces he had on him all the time: sugar packets, salt packets, paper serviettes, tape measure, Jack's metal spoon, plastic spoons, two cigarette lighters, penknife, extra elastic bands, sauce packets, towel scrap, Jack's holdall (bigger and tougher than a plastic bag), plastic bags, biros, crisp packets (empty), Jack's lead (a *proper* one too, not a tatty bit of string), chewing-gum (chewed and unchewed), a pack of dog Top Trumps (best of breed) and his receipts. They weren't *his* receipts. He just collected them, went looking for them on the ground, sometimes fished them out of bins. He read them out of curiosity to see what it was that people bought in shops, but the reason he kept them was in case he was ever caught *outside* a shop with something he hadn't paid for. And then if the guard marched him back inside he could say, "But I've got a receipt, mate." And see how long they spent looking through that lot before they let him off. That was the idea, anyway.

He examined his plastic spoons and threw away some with splits in, flicking them all into the road and a couple of the biros too. One of the zombies gave him a backwards glance, twisted her mouth a bit and then looked away. He got out his Oyster card from the little pocket near the collar of his coat. He'd found it by one of the machines when the cold had driven him down into the tunnels to ride the Circle line. It was a while since he'd used up the credit and he looked at it as if it was no longer his. He put it back and got his red penknife out. It was his prize possession and he held it in his palm to admire it. Inside were two blades: one big, one small. On the outside was a compass that told you where you were going. And it didn't matter how fast you turned round trying to trick it, it always went back to pointing north and never let you down. He'd robbed it from a climbing shop. The small blade he used for little odd jobs like cutting up plastic containers for Jack to drink from. The big blade he saved to keep it sharp. He'd never done anything with it except to wave it at an older boy as he was running away.

He put his penknife back in his jeans and carried on looking, hoping to find a coin, a note, anything with a face on it, and he was almost finished now, pulling things out and putting them away. Finally then, to wrap things up, he got out his card. All the corners were bashed in so that it didn't look like a card any more but he could still see what it said on the front. There was a picture of a face – a lady's face, he'd decided, though it had just a squiggle of hair – whispering to someone inside the card. It made you want to open it. But he didn't, not yet. He read the words on the front first, like you were supposed to. He always read the words.

I've got something to tell you...

He moved away from the railings, further back from the road, and opened it up. The face on the front was the same face inside but much bigger with a real-looking mouth cut into the card and a red paper tongue. And he concentrated on the words that were going to come out of this mouth.

... I love you ... I love you so much ... I love you more than ... more than anyone ... more than anything else in the world... Happy Birthday, Bradley! Happy birthday, love... Lots and lots and lots of love from your mummy...

And then the best bit, the bit he always waited for at the end: the kisses.

Mmpur, mmpurrr, mmpurr... Mmmmmrrr...

Her voice was beginning to sound a bit Dalek-y, like the

batteries were starting to go, and he wondered if he should stop doing this every time he went through his pockets.

Bully looked around and one of the zombies waiting at the lights was smiling at him with pity eyes. He gave her a murderous look and clapped the card shut. As he did he heard a little *plinky* noise above the traffic. He opened the card back up and it said nothing. He frantically flapped it open and closed a couple of times before he could accept it was broken. Something had fallen *out*. He swore a lot and bent down, scanning the pavement, waving a fresh pile of zombies away like it was a crime scene.

He saw the little roundness of the battery sitting on the pavement and he picked it up very carefully with the tips of his fingers. The slot where it went must be somewhere inside the card. He put his fingers in the mouth and felt something crinkly behind the paper tongue. It wasn't money: too papery, too thin. It *looked* like a receipt when he pulled it out, but when he unfolded it he saw it was just a lottery ticket.

It must have got stuck there somehow. He didn't remember finding it. Still, worth checking it out, and it would take his mind off thinking about the money he'd lost to the river.

05 **04** **35**
DAYS HOURS MINUTES

The girl at the till inside the station scanned his ticket without interest.

She was new. He knew all the staff by sight. She stopped what she was doing and pulled a face like the ticket had broken something in the machine.

"Gra-ham…" she said and Bully palmed a packet of chewing-gum for the fraction of a second she turned her head. An older man came to the till. Bully got ready to run.

"Graham, what does this mean? *Contact Camelot, Watford?*" She pointed to the screen.

"Oh, right," he said and gave her a little nod to say he was taking over. Bully craned his neck to see and when he caught the girl's eyes again she was looking at him differently, as if he was someone she thought she should recognize.

"What? Does it say I won a tenner?"

"No… It's not that…" said the manager man and Bully swore and began to walk away.

"Heh, no! Hold on a sec—"

Bully turned round and the man surprised him, holding the ticket out, and looking concerned.

"You've won a lot more than *that*."

"How much is more than *that* then?" The girl smirked and Bully gave her a look.

"I don't know, I can't say, but it's not an instant cash prize. It's not something we can pay out of the till. It's too much," the manager added when he saw the boy's face. "That's all I can tell you really. We just have to go by what's on the screen."

Bully thought about that. How much was too much for the till? He'd seen wads of tens and twenties when they opened it up to give change … must be at least three or four hundred quid in there … maybe a thousand or *more*.

"This is your ticket, is it, then?" The man had pulled a look over his face, tried to make it sound like he was just asking, like he didn't really care.

"Yeah … someone else bought it though," Bully said, in case he didn't believe a boy like him could afford to be buying tickets. And then he remembered. It must be *that* ticket. And the memory of it, suddenly sharp in his head after all these months, started to hurt again and work him up. He looked round the busy shop to make sure of his exit.

"Well, someone needs to phone the number on the ticket…" The man slowly handed it back to him. "Or we can phone from here, if you like? If you've got I.D.?"

"Nah, it's OK," Bully said. He didn't want anyone turning up and asking questions, all sorts of questions.

"You'd better get moving—"

Bully cut him off. "I'm going, all right!" he said, misunderstanding the man's tone.

"No, the ticket, I mean. There's a claim limit on it."

"What? You only just looked at it!" Trying to rip him off.

"No, it starts from the date of the draw … 180 days … there, see?" The man leaned over the counter and pointed out the faint date on the ticket. "That's February the 16th," he said as if Bully was stupid. Bully knew what day that was, didn't need to look at the numbers to know that day.

"Are you sure you don't want me to phone Camelot for you?"

Bully shook his head like he was Jack with a rat in her mouth and then when he was sure he'd said no, out came a question.

"What happens to it then – to the winnings – if no one phones up in time?"

"Well…" the manager man said, considering it. "I'm not sure but I think it just goes back into the prize fund or to charity or something."

To *charity*? Why would they want to go and do that? Waste all his money on little kids and wheelchairs.

The man carried on talking but Bully wasn't listening now. He was looking at his ticket. What day was it, today? He looked at the green numbers on the till screen. *6.45 p.m.* it said one side, *09/08/13* on the other. What day was *that* though? All of a sudden he couldn't understand what the numbers meant. He *was* stupid.

He turned round and looked at one of the papers to give him a proper day with a name to it. Today was Friday. And it was the 9th of August. He counted the months out on his fingers from February to August. It was nearly six months. So how many days was that? There were some months with more days than others in them and he tried to get a rusted-up rhyme going in his head. February had 28 days except in a leap year, he knew that.

He looked at today's date again. It was too complicated to work out so he just did six thirties to average it out. But he couldn't do that either. So he tried six threes instead which was eighteen and then added a zero. That was 180 already!

He was frightened then that he'd run out of time.

But the man was smiling at him. "It's five days you've got – well, six if you include what's left of today – that's how long you've got left on the ticket," he said. He leaned over the till and the look on his face changed: like he wanted to tell him something that he didn't have to, that wasn't part of his job.

"And I'd keep it quiet if I was you … until someone puts your claim in at Camelot…"

2

05 **04** **30**
DAYS HOURS MINUTES

Still in the station, Bully looked at his ticket again, at the numbers. He remembered buying it for his mum a couple of days before she died. She must have put it in his card and tucked it inside the paper mouth because she wasn't thinking straight on all the drugs.

He put the ticket away inside his top pocket with his Oyster card and went back to thinking about his winnings piled up in pound coins in Camelot, in Watford. He looked back at the shop, at the sign for the lottery outside. It was a picture of fingers crossed for luck with a stupid smile creased underneath. He knew the sign for the lottery used to be a man on a horse. And he thought about this knight inside a castle looking after this money that didn't fit in the till. He could do with some of it now, he was starving – that pain in his guts starting up again like roadworks. He might pick up something off the tables along the river or try the bins outside the station. There were eating places he went to inside the station but he preferred to be outside if the weather was good.

He walked towards the side exit, through a smaller arch

where the taxis picked up passengers. He kept close to the walls, out the way of the CCTV. He didn't like the idea of people looking at him, looking *for* him maybe, though he doubted it. Phil couldn't wait for him to leave the flat after his mum died, had never liked having him around in the first place. And Phil didn't like dogs, either. It was only down to his mum that he had been allowed to keep Jack when he brought her home from the shopping-centre car park, after grabbing her with one hand from underneath that 4x4.

He was deep, deep down in his thoughts when his eyes dragged him back to the surface to see what he was seeing: dead ahead of him were Feds, real Feds this time, wriggling around the punters at the taxi rank.

Bully turned on his heels. And then, walking away from the taxi rank, he ducked left into Burger King, his stomach taking over the thinking in this emergency. As he went in he pulled out a crinkled-up holdall from one of his big coat pockets. He let it skim the ground for a second, didn't have to say a word and Jack jumped in.

"Shh," he said and got his scrap of towel out and laid it over Jack's head.

He went straight upstairs, avoiding the eyes of the Whopper boys on the tills. (If you looked at them, they looked at you.) The first thing he did before scouting for leftovers was go to the toilets. The first thing he did in the toilets was to go to the toilet. He only went for a sit-down every three or four days. Personally, that suited him. He didn't like *having* to sit still for five, ten minutes. It was like being back at school, waiting for the end to come... And ten, fifteen minutes later the end did come ... job done.

The second thing he did was refill his water bottle. You could live months without food but only days without water. Phil used to go on about it back at the flat: running out of rat packs away from base was no problem – you lost a few kilograms maybe – but you did not want to run out of water *in the field*. No way. Though all the time Phil had lived with them Bully had never seen him drink water in the flat, let alone in a field.

"He's like a human camel," Bully's mum used to say before Phil came back to the flat with a big hole in his back like a mushroom growing the wrong way. And after that, no one talked about camels any more.

He washed his hands and dried them properly like he was doing an operation. He was fixing his card so it could talk again. It was a very fiddly thing to do without ruining the mechanism but he managed to fit the little battery back in the slot inside the face. He opened up the card; it didn't speak. He swore a bit, then, remembering about pluses and minuses, he took the battery out and turned it round and tried it again and finally heard what he needed to hear.

He sighed, got the gut shakes he was so hungry now and put the card away. Getting ready to leave he looked in the mirror and saw this scraggy, spindle-shanked boy giving him a "what d'you want?" face.

He leaned in towards the glass. He could see where his hat had been these last few warm weeks because the top of his forehead was paler than the rest of his skin. Where the sun had got to him he was very brown but his cheeks underneath were still showing red. His mum said it was because people pinched them when he was a baby because he was so cute but he didn't believe that. And he had large eyes that were still no better for seeing with and lips that looked kind of blubbery, like someone had caught him a sucker punch a few days ago. He wished he had spots. They made you look older because they left little scars.

He caught himself rubbing his top lip to see if it was just dirt stuck there. And though it was just dirt, he definitely still looked sixteen. Maybe seventeen, he thought, and he spiked his hair to make up for the lost centimetres but it was too greasy and fell flat.

Jack whimpered and started scrabbling up his knees with her huggy legs because she was hungry too but you couldn't let a dog do that to you.

"Get down ... down. Now, OK, all right, cut it out, mate. I already told you we're getting something to eat. Don't be so impatient," he said, making a big deal of it because he felt guilty. Jack was getting bigger too and needed more food than Bully was giving her.

He opened the toilet door and had a scout about the eating place. One of the Whopper girls was cleaning the tables. Bully waited for her to go back downstairs. As soon as he heard her shoes clacking he came out and sat down at his favoured table and plugged his mobile into the mains that the cleaners used. The battery in the phone wasn't much good now. Even if he turned it off, it still died on him after a few days. After he phoned up Camelot, he'd buy a new one with his five hundred quid or however much it was that was too much for the till. One you could play proper games on.

He looked round to see what there was to eat. Upstairs was getting to be quieter in the summer evening times and there was just an old man eating every bit on his tray and a mum and dad with two kids messing about with their chips, their free toys still wrapped up new. The mum and dad looked at him suspiciously but the kids didn't notice he was there. When they left he sidled over to their table, keeping an eye out for the manager, for the Feds, for anyone who didn't like the look of him. He took the tray, stashed the ketchup sachets to eat later, ate the chips, and with a huge effort of self-control, he lifted up the towel and slipped Jack the bits of burger.

"I spoil you," he said, like his mum used to say to him.

His phone beeped back on. A shot of Jack when she was little with a long white snout lit up the screen. When his mum was still alive, his wallpaper used to be a selfie his mum had taken of them with her arms round his neck. She was wearing a funny hat in the photo to cover her empty head, funny because she never wore hats. But he'd deleted that one a while ago because he didn't want to think of her like that, wearing a hat.

His credit came up as zero. He needed credit to ring Camelot. He pictured the castle, this time with water all the way round and knights on motorbikes instead of horses, riding round with machine guns, guarding his winnings.

He heard feet on the stairs, got ready to dip into the toilets but it was just a geeky zombie with a laptop. He looked too happy to be anyone official, too relaxed, and Bully decided he could risk it. He put on his best voice, the one he used for questions and favours.

"Where's Watford, mate?"

"Sorry?"

"Watford, mate. How far is it, mate?"

"Umm, well, I don't really know. It's sort of North London, north *of* London. It must be near Hemel Hempstead… Rickmansworth way…"

He didn't need teaching about it, just telling. Maybe this guy, maybe he was a teacher.

"How far is it?"

"I don't know – about twenty-odd miles."

"So you could walk there then?"

"I suppose you could. You'd have to really want to, though." He puffed out a laugh but Bully just nodded.

"Yeah," he said, because he might have to walk it if he couldn't beg any money or jump a train and risk losing one of his five days stuck answering questions if he was caught.

Bully got ready to go but then he had another think. Maybe if he went online it might tell him exactly how much he'd won. How much was too much for the till.

"You look up my numbers on your laptop?"

The man hesitated to say yes but didn't say no or shake his head.

"Sorry, what numbers?"

"The lottery. The numbers. Not this week's. I don't want them."

"No, OK, but I don't know if I can get a connection in here…" the man said, putting his hand on the screen and looking down at the floor to make sure his satchel was still there and then seeing Jack's head poking out. He flinched, sat up straight.

"Is he all right in there?"

"Dudn't *live* in there, mate."

The man relaxed a little. "Oh, OK. Your dog, is it?"

Who else's dog was she going to be, sitting there next to him being fed bits of burger? Why did people keep asking him that? Like he'd nicked her from a blind man or something. Jack was as good as any dopey Labrador. She could lead you anywhere whether you had any eyes or not.

"Yeah. It's *my* dog," he said, just about controlling himself enough to be patient with another zombie asking stupid questions about his dog.

"Oh, OK. Cool, nice dog." He opened the laptop up and tapped the keys. The guy didn't know anything about dogs, Bully could tell.

"OK… So when was it, the draw then? Which week are we after?"

What did he mean, *we*? Bully didn't like the sound of that, like he was looking to get something out of this for himself just for tapping the keys. Bully got his ticket out and read the date of the draw and the man put it into the Camelot website and then twisted the laptop round to show him the results. Bully leaned closer, his lips working, mumbling to himself but not saying anything just like the beggar man on the bridge. And for close to a minute he read the numbers right to left, left to right, comparing them with the random ones on his ticket he had out underneath the table.

The man was beginning to get uneasy again.

"Any good?"

"No … no. No good. Gotta go," he said and stood up, unplugged his mobile and picked up Jack.

"Look, do you want this? I'm not that hungry. I just got it for the drink really." The man was handing him his burger, still in the wrapper, as good as throwing it away. Bully took it, tore off half and swallowed it before he got to the bottom of the stairs. And though he was starving he'd had a job to force it down because he'd been calculating (the best bit of maths he'd ever done) how many millions of meals he could buy just like it and still have spare change.

05 04 02
DAYS HOURS MINUTES

Because he had all the numbers. All six. He had won it, the big one. The one people went mad about. The jackpot. He couldn't remember exactly how much but it was more than a million. It was always *millions*.

Why hadn't the manager man in Smiths just told him so? Didn't want to go shouting out his numbers, everyone crowding round, maybe. But then he remembered nothing had come up on the screen because he'd been looking at it. *Contact Camelot, Watford …* that was all it said. The manager man *knew* he'd won big. He just didn't know how big.

There must have been something about it on the news back in the winter, but then he hadn't heard any news since they'd left the flat. And though he sometimes watched TV through the shop windows on the Strand and on the big giant screen above the platforms at Waterloo, it was all silent news. And he didn't *read* news. The only thing he read was magazines.

"We won it, mate … we won it," he said to Jack but it still didn't make it real enough. He buzzed around for a while with the notion that he was rich, proper rich like off the TV with enough cash to buy things, not just a few things but *every* thing he wanted. And he had the rest of the night, and another five days if he felt like it, to feel like *this*, that feeling of looking forward to something.

He wanted to tell someone. He *needed* to. The urge was strong, like a nice hunger. The manager man in Smiths had told him not to but he was talking about someone he didn't know, wasn't he? So Bully weaselled his way back out of the station, through the arch, down past the dead train drivers' steps, back towards the river, looking for a face he knew. There was no one around on his side, just the eaters in the eating places and the skateboarders pushing out onto the pavements, getting braver now the sun was going, doing tricks on the benches and rails.

So he crossed the footbridge, put his hands to his ears as he hurried past the guys playing trumpets, thumping their big plastic cans for money. They were there most nights in the summer but he never hung around to listen, didn't like that noise. Lots of noises he didn't like, but over to his left he didn't mind the big clock, Big Ben, by the politicians' place that was going *bang, bang, bang* … for nine o'clock, because he knew what that meant. It was the time.

Even so, he looked away to his right along the river, at the other buildings stacked up against the water, some of them stone, some of them glass, one of them like a huge sharp lump of ice. And further down the river, the skyscraper like a giant bullet, and the skinny bridge and the big church looking like a blurry ice-cream cone that somebody had just wasted and thrown away.

He walked on up to the square, let Jack size up the dirty brown lions lounging around Nelson's Column. He wondered what the little man with the pointy hat could see up there. Maybe the bridge at the end of the river that opened up for the boats to go under. He didn't have the nerve yet to travel that far away. He liked to stick to the patch he'd got to know. Along the Strand, up Kingsway, down Charing Cross and the Haymarket and then back across the river to the Eye was as far as Bully went. A lopsided square of roads, shops and offices that he had somehow in the last five and a half months decided was his territory, his own bit of turf.

He was going to the Strand now. The punters would be about, fagging outside the theatre places, and he might pick up a couple of quid to top up his mobile. There were a lot of these theatre places along the Strand and he sometimes looked at the posters they put up and watched the lights flashing for the shows. Back at the flat, Phil, when he was wasted, used to talk about the *theatre of war*, but it wasn't like one of these theatre places where they acted things out and did a song and dance for money. Phil said they shot each other instead.

He wandered along with Jack, in a world of his own, thinking about what he would buy from the shops on his way back from Camelot in Watford. He wanted a games console – an Xbox, the new one, and a PlayStation, but not the Wii – that was for kids… He looked in a shop window at the dumb show on all the TVs. Yeah, and a big, big plasma 52 inch, maybe 62, maybe a hundred! No, better than that, he'd have a screen built into one of the walls… He would need walls for that though. So maybe he would have to get a place first for all this stuff he was going to buy.

He heard a sharp whistle – the sort he had never learned to make, with two fingers in your back teeth.

"Bully!"

A couple of zombies outside the theatre place looked round, thinking something was up, but it was just his name. Bully for bulldog, like his dog – like some of his dog, anyway.

"Bully, Bully! You all righ'!" The two Sammies came over, hanging off each other, laughing and falling about like they were in a three-legged race and close to coming last.

Man Sammy bent down to make a fuss of Jack, the other

Sammy, a big old lady one, kissing Bully on the lips.

"You all righ', love," she said, draping one arm round him like she was fed up with holding it herself. Close up she looked older than last time he'd seen her, like she was her own sister. Bully smelled the drink, and her eyes were slow to look at him. He didn't like drink. He'd tried it – course he had – but it tasted like medicine and why would he want to take medicine when there was nothing wrong with him?

"We been Sunderlan', haven't we, Sam?" said the other Sammy.

Man Sammy ignored her, playing with Jack, tickling her belly. "Bite me? You gunna bite me, eh? Who's a nasty dog, eh? Who's a nasty dog?"

"D'you hitch?" Bully asked. He didn't like it when Man Sammy said things like that to his dog like she was a bad dog.

"On the coach, love."

He wondered how they got their money. Neither one of them did much begging as far as he could tell.

"You seen Tiggs and Chris?" he asked. It was where they came from, *up north*, and he took it for granted that everyone that way sort of knew what everyone else was up to.

"Nah. Dunno where they are. Up to their eyeballs in it, I expect…" Man Sammy put a finger to his eyelid and dragged it down so that Bully could see his whole eye shining in its socket.

He heard a bell tinkling inside the theatre place and one or two zombies started doing a little twisty dance on their cigarettes whilst the rest headed back to their seats. Bully spread out on the empty steps and listened to the rest of what the two Sammies had to say. Then he told them about Janks.

"He loves his taxin', always, always … taxin' us," said Man Sammy.

"Yeah, but it's never you's has to pay," said the other Sammy, pulling a face, and Man Sammy told her to *shut it* and to keep it like that. And then they agreed that the river would be better off without Janks – who didn't even live on the streets but in a house, partying all night, and who didn't need the money – giving the pavement a bad name, taxing for the fun of it, for the *laughs*.

The other Sammy draped both her arms around Bully so that they were now like a little noose of bones and flesh around his neck.

"Little boy I never had," she said.

"Get off him!" said Man Sammy but her arms stayed where they were.

The last of the zombies left to go back inside, and no one said anything for a while. Bully could feel his news working its way out.

"I won it," he said.

"Won what?" said the other Sammy dreamily. "What you won, love?"

"The lottery. I won it!"

"What?" Man Sammy's voice sharpened up. "How much?"

"All of it," he whispered, almost to himself, so that he was surprised when he heard Man Sammy making fun of him.

"You *ain't* won it! You *ain't* won nothin'! You'd be on the telly!"

"In't 'e *sweet*," said the other Sammy.

"I haven't told 'em yet, have I? And I'm not having no publicity anyway!" This was something he'd just decided. He didn't like having his picture taken since his mum had stopped taking it.

"Course you did, love," said the other Sammy, giving him another kiss. He tried to pull away without upsetting her because it was sore from where Janks had throttled him. "Where you going?" she said, giggling as if it was a game. And he ducked his head out from under her arms.

"I got all the numbers!" Man Sammy's voice squeaked and crackled as he tried to make it go all high, making fun of Bully's voice that was changing all the time.

Bully stood up. "I have, I got all six! They scanned it and everything. And I'm going to Camelot to get it! In Watford!" he added, to show how true it was, because Watford was a real place.

Man Sammy stopped laughing and his face closed down and his eyes searched Bully's for a few seconds before he spoke. "Let's have a little look-see then, at this little ticket of yours," he said quietly. And Bully realized he'd said way too much.

"I ain't got it with me, have I? Got it stashed…" He tapped his little finger against his coat pocket to signal Jack he was ready to go. Jack was on her back though, still having her belly rubbed.

"Where you put it then?"

"Left it in the lockers…" Bully whistled softly with a bit of breath he was blowing out anyway and Jack rolled onto her feet, back on duty.

"What lockers? There's no lockers at Waterloo."

"What? Yeah, yeah, no. Not *there*."

"Where? Where's the *key* then?"

He made a show of patting his coat down like he was looking for it. "Dunno… Look, we gotta go. Got stuff to do. Yeah, laters." And he was padding across the Strand, Jack at his heels, before either of the Sammies got to their feet.

"Bully, love, don't go!" shouted the other Sammy but he didn't look back – ran straight in front of a bus, just making it across, Jack a little ahead of him, knowing the way. And they kept the pace up between them, across the footbridge, back past the guys still playing their trumpets and drums for money, back towards Waterloo where the sun was just beginning to think about bedding down for the night.

3

04 **23** **21**
DAYS HOURS MINUTES

He didn't like being out and about when the sun played hide-and-seek. He wasn't one for roaming after dark. He liked to get organized, get settled for the night. A lot of the older boys liked the empty hours, owning the streets for a while before the day brought the zombies back to town. But Bully didn't. It wasn't the dark itself. There was plenty of light around at night in London. No, what he didn't like about the night-time was the people who came out of it. The way they went nasty and did things they wouldn't do in the day. So he always laid out his cardboard bedding and his blankets and sleeping bag on his doorway before the sun went down.

The step that he slept on was at the back of an alleyway, a nice little dead-end off Old Paradise Street, not far from the station, past a little row of shops with a dancing lady painted on the end of the brick wall. She had a bowl of bananas and oranges and pineapples balanced on her head and Bully gauged how hungry he was by if he ever walked past and even *thought* about eating fruit.

There were no cars parked in his alleyway. The only thing it was good for was rubbish. Two metal bins as big as cars took up most of the space. Even so, when the rubbish truck came reversing in from the main road on Tuesday nights, he made sure his wheelie bin (that he'd nicked) with all his bedding in was tucked out the way. He didn't want to have to go looking for new blankets at night.

He'd been lucky to get it. The first night in town he'd spent wandering around the station. On his second night he was so tired he'd fallen asleep on the steps where the names of the dead train drivers were written into the walls. *COMPANY EMPLOYEES WHO GAVE THEIR LIVES IN THE GREAT WAR* it said in the stone.

Alfred Appleby
John Ardle
James Bootle...

He tried to remember which war was the great one, that was so *big*, that everybody got so excited about. It said *1914–1918* on the wall but he wasn't sure if that was the one with Hitler in or not.

Phil had told him that in the army the fighting bit, the war bit, was OK, as long as you were pulling the trigger and doing something. And that gave you a bit of a rush, getting away with it for another day, but he'd never said any of it was *great*. And Bully had drifted off that second night thinking about all those dead train drivers driving *ghost* trains after their war and was nearly caught by the Feds.

It was Chris who had saved him. He'd seen the Feds on their way, come over and given him a tap and got him and Jack moving. Bully'd wandered around for the rest of the night with Tiggs and Chris, in and out of takeaways to keep warm, and in the morning he'd gone round the back of McDonald's with Jack and found this place.

He lay down on his step. The doorway was too small and the step too narrow for a big man or even an older boy of much more than five feet and a half to bed down on, and his cardboard crinkled out over the edge. He didn't know where the door went. No one had opened it while he was there, not while he was awake, anyway. There was no name or number on it, just a keypad, and sometimes he'd punch in numbers to see if he could get it to open. So far, he'd had no luck.

"What's this?" he said, picking fluff from his sleeping bag out of Jack's coarse fur. "There's a bit of poodle in you, mate." He thought this was really hilarious and said it most nights even if he couldn't find any fluff.

What he spent most of his time picking out of Jack's coat though was *fleas*. His eyesight was good enough close up. The warm weather the past few days had been breeding them up and yesterday he'd squished thirteen between his nails so that his fingers looked like they were bleeding. The thought of it had Bully checking Jack's ear. The tear was ragged like a torn ticket and he rubbed a bit of his own spit into it for good measure, though human spit did nothing for dogs.

Jack whined a little and then nuzzled up to him. Her dog tag touched his sore skin. And because it was metal it felt cold even though the night was warm. He scratched under her jaw with one hand and with the other rubbed the little brass disc between his fingers. His mum had paid out extra to have it engraved and he traced the letters of the name cut into the metal. It reminded Bully of his money.

Jack suddenly twitched away from him and started up, pointing towards the bins. Her growl ticked over.

Rats.

A small one had got into his sleeping bag in the winter and bitten his ear. Bully had woken up screaming to see Jack shaking her head like she was saying *no, no, no* to the rat in her mouth.

He was about to put Jack on it when there was a *beep, beep, beep* from the emergency exit at the back of McDonald's. One of the burger boys was dumping the trash. It was twenty-four hour opening and this went on through the night. The alarm used to wake him up when he first moved in but nowadays most of the time he slept through it. Sometimes early in the morning he went looking for food in the bins, but he didn't like climbing in there with all those black bags bobbling about and maybe rats trapped in there in the darkness with him too.

When the door shut and the alarm stopped Jack settled down and the rat was gone. Bully got out his Top Trumps. He'd remembered to bring them with him when they left the flat. He went through them most nights, working out what Jack was from the pictures and descriptions of the different breeds. The categories were *height, weight, guard-dog skill, rarity* and *lovability*. Jack didn't do so well on height or weight, losing out to the big hounds, but she made up for it in the other three categories. Though Jack's breed wasn't exactly in the pack, Bully was sure there were bits of her in among all those pedigrees and most nights he went searching for exactly what mixture of dogs she was. A bit of red setter, maybe, around her neck, and the way she sometimes pointed like a gundog with her long nose. Or ... maybe Jack was crossed with something much, much bigger and she was just the runt of the litter. This was the first time he had thought this up. Maybe she was part English mastiff or Great Dane. They were big dogs, bigger than men and real breeds too, with proper *ancestors* and *lineage*. The dog magazines said so. It was something to think about.

A while later, he put the pack of dogs away and tried to get to sleep but he was too excited. Every time he drifted off, thoughts started frothing up about what he would buy with his cash. Somewhere to live first of all. A penthouse flat right at the top of a block where you could scout everything out, nice and quiet with a swimming pool all to himself and no screaming kids. But would a penthouse be big enough for all his stuff? Maybe he'd just get a house, then, not joined up to next door but one on its own with a garden. A big, big house with lots of windows so he could see what was coming from miles away. And the roof would be made of glass too so that when he looked up he could see the planes and the sky. And it would have security alarms and razor wire and an electric fence to electrocute the scumbags who deserved it. And it would be where all the footballers lived. And all the rooms would have fridges full of cold cans of Coke. And it would have beds. Just normal-sized beds though, like the one he had back at the flat. That would do him. And Jack could have her own room full of squeaky toys and sticks and cans of food without *any* ash in them at all. He'd pay someone to pick it out.

He got out his lottery ticket to look at it again, to make sure it was still real. He read the numbers. Then he turned the ticket over to read the back.

Game rules…

The tiny red print was difficult to read in the shadows. He got out a cigarette lighter and scanned the print through the top of the yellow flame. Some of the words sounded foreign – what were *aspects*? Was *amended* something that had been mended? It didn't matter. He had the numbers. And he still had five days. He would phone them up tomorrow. Camelot at Watford. Get some credit or use a payphone. And then he would go get his millions. The drawbridge would come down and they would let him into Camelot, this castle place, and the knights would show him the money. He knew it wouldn't really be like that but he liked to think of it that way all the same.

He was down to the second-but-last one of the rules and the flint of the lighter was beginning to hot up his fingers.

It is illegal for any person under sixteen to buy tickets or claim prizes.

He'd never thought about the rules. He'd looked at them on the backs of the tickets before but he'd never *thought* about them, what it meant when he bought a ticket for his mum, Old Mac at the till turning a blind eye as long as you were in his shop. And just in case he hadn't understood, there at the bottom was a red circle with *15* inside, crossed out.

He dropped the lighter.

He was too young to play.

04 **17** **03**
DAYS HOURS MINUTES

All night he spent making plans, dozing off then waking up with a jolt whenever the burger boys dumped rubbish. A couple of times he got up and swore loudly enough to make it echo in the alleyway. Eventually, like a lesson at school with a strict teacher, he settled down to doing what he was supposed to, which was working out how to get his money. There was no name on the ticket. Nothing on it but his numbers and the date he'd bought it – like a receipt; *proof of purchase* but no proof of *who* purchased. If he couldn't claim his prize because he was too young to play then he would have to find someone who was old enough to claim it for him.

By the time the sun found the alleyway he'd drawn up a list in his head of people he could trust. It was a short list because at the top of it had to be someone he could trust to take his money and then give it back to him. There had only ever been one person at the top of the list but she couldn't help him out. Chris was second from the top and Tiggs maybe further down but neither of them were about, so the two Sammies said. And suddenly he didn't trust either of the Sammies. Third on his list was Kevin, but he'd gone back to live with his mum on the Isle of Dogs (wherever that was). So, fourth on the list was Stan. He was old enough, Bully was sure he was, and he was always around across the river. He went to text him but remembered he still didn't have any credit. He thought about begging for a few quid but he wanted to get started, get across the river and think about it then. And someone would know where Stan was anyway, it was like that on the pavement. Someone knew someone who knew the someone you were after, and you could find anyone that way without any credit on your phone.

He walked down Old Paradise Street, towards the river, every so often Jack rolling in the sunshine, scratching at a fresh batch of fleas. Bully stopped at the dual carriageway with the crash barriers and railings that ran alongside the river. There was an old tunnel that ran parallel with the road. He'd followed it over ground and it came out near the station further downstream. It used to be for cars but now it was just for the zombies.

He never went down there though, even when it was raining. Even in the day with the strip lighting and the sun digging away at the edges of the darkness, he didn't like being *under* the ground if he could help it. It made him think about his mum and where he'd left her.

After she'd died, Phil had brought her back to the flat in a big plastic sweetie jar. What the fire left behind when they burnt you up. He knew you were supposed to scatter the ashes but when they went missing without any ceremony

Bully had his *suspicions* that they had not been scattered but *thrown away*, which was not the same thing at all.

He'd found them in one of the big bins at the bottom of the rubbish chute that served their landing. He didn't say anything to Phil but kept them under his bed in the sweetie jar for two days. And then when he left the flat, he took them with him. He'd planned to do the job himself, scatter them into the river on the way to the train station because his mum had always wanted to go on a boat on a cruise. But when it came to it, he couldn't bear to get rid of her like that, seeing her for the last time, shaking her out in the cold, in the winter time, and watching her sink to the bottom of the river. So, just with his hands, he'd buried the jar for safekeeping in a bit of dirt the council never got round to filling in with flowers. He'd marked the spot with a piece of broken paving-stone. When he got his money, he would go back and dig her up and take her on a cruise to the Caribbean and scatter her somewhere nice and warm.

When he got down to his own river he went over the footbridge. When they were nearly across Jack squatted down, shivered, doing a big one. A woman on her own coming towards him stopped when she saw what Jack was doing and screwed up her make-up face like she couldn't understand what it was coming out of Jack's rear end.

"Are you going to pick that up?" she said, a safe distance away.

Bully flicked the Vs at her, told her his dog had to go somewhere, didn't she? And then he told her where to go and how to get there. And when Jack was done, he didn't pick it up – that *was* disgusting – and they carried on across to the other side of the water.

He had a good look round for Stan in Trafalgar Square and along the Strand. It was still early though, shops just pulling their shutters up and a few men still sleeping in one or two of the doorways, their heads hiding from the light. Most of the doorways were empty and wet. It hadn't rained. They'd been washed last night. The washermen only did it on the Strand and a few of the other big streets where the zombies spent most of their time walking up and down. He'd heard the Daveys complaining about it – *hot washing* they called it; get you up and start you talking first, they did, with a nice hot cup of tea and filling in forms, while a washerman hoses your doorway down behind your back, soaking your cardboard for the night. And Bully walked on through Covent Garden, feeling lucky that he had the luxury of a dry step every night. He traipsed around the bumpy streets looking for something to eat, yawning and scratching his head because the morning sun made it itch. He didn't give the meal in the morning a name any more. It was just time to eat when he was hungry and that was most of the time.

He patted his top pocket with the lottery ticket in as he walked, keeping an eye out for delivery trucks that pulled up outside the little supermarkets. Sometimes if they left the back open you could fish out a packet or a tin. Once he had got hold of a *fish* with a tail and silvery scales and frozen eyes but he couldn't sell it or cook it so he'd carried it back as far as the river and then lobbed it off the bridge. It made a splash like a real live one going back into the water.

When Bully got as far up as Shaftesbury Avenue he stopped. And though it was OK to cross, buses and taxis just toddling along in the early morning emptiness of a Saturday, he just stood and stared at the road. He didn't normally go any further than this. It was like a river to him, in his head anyway, like there was dirty, dark water running between the kerbs. The problem was, Stan liked to hang out around Soho on the other side. And though he needed Stan's help, Bully turned back towards Covent Garden to wait a while on his own side.

He spotted a Davey looking for fresh cardboard in the rubbish the shops put out. He kept pulling at bits, testing them for quality, seeing how thick they were. Bully approached him warily, as if he were a breed of dog he wasn't sure how to deal with.

"All right, mate. You seen Stan?"

"Keep that dog off me! Keep it away."

"She won't hurt you." The Davey twitched his nose, wasn't so sure. And the man's fear made Bully feel more confident about his questions. "So you seen him or what?"

"You got a loosey, pal?" he asked, as if pricing up what he had to say.

"Nah, mate." Bully patted his pockets to show that he didn't have anything to smoke and the old man crouched down and began scouring the pavement and gutters for ciggy butts. Bully watched him tear a Subway wrapper into strips, then open up all the ends of the butts he'd found with the edge of his fingernail and sprinkle the tobacco onto the paper, conjuring a fag from nothing. Bully's mum never smoked, not in the flat, but Phil did, and there were little brown patches on the ceilings above the end of the sofa and the kettle in the kitchen. Bully had tried ciggies, real ones out of a packet. He didn't like them – the feeling of the smoke cramping his lungs. And Bully didn't do much he didn't like.

"So you seen him then or not, mate?"

"Stan? No… I seen Mick though." Bully nodded. Mick was an old, old Davey. For a few years he'd had a flat all to himself in Hammersmith but couldn't get used to it – complained there were too many walls. So he'd started back on the pavement and that's when Mick had palled up with Stan. It was like him and Jack, keeping an eye out for each other, though Bully didn't trust Mick; he wasn't anywhere on his list.

"So where is he then?" Bully said, getting to the end of his patience, not so afraid of this Davey now because he was keeping still, sitting on the kerb.

"He's kipping round the back of Hanways."

"What? Where's that?"

"You boys get lost turning round. Off Oxford Street."

"Yeah, yeah, I know it," he said, though it wasn't near his territory.

"You got a light?" asked the Davey.

"No," said Bully reflexively but then pulled out one of his lighters. He wouldn't be needing it. He could buy a billion lighters now and millions and millions of fags and maybe he'd give them all to Phil to smoke himself to death.

"Have it." He chucked the lighter and the old man caught it but carried on staring at him.

"You the boy with the ticket?"

"What?" Bully froze.

"You 'im? That's your dog, innit?"

The shock of his own news coming out of the old man's mouth made him feel sick.

"Not me, mate," he said. Jack sensed the change in Bully's voice and growled at the man, gave him the front teeth stare.

"Lend us a few quid," the old man pleaded, holding out both his hands, dropping the lighter. He started shouting, swearing at Bully's back as he ran away.

The few people watching in Covent Garden might have thought it was an act; this boy punching himself in the arm and the neck, like he was trying to beat himself up. No one threw any money at him though. He stopped and got his breath back. Should have kept his mouth shut yesterday. He needed to think about this now, what he would say if anyone else came up to him asking questions. He would deny he was the boy but he couldn't say Jack wasn't *that* dog. There wasn't another like her, with that head full of teeth and those funny front legs that reminded Bully of a little kid he'd once seen trying to carry a ten pin bowling ball. In truth they both stuck out; they didn't fit in. He would have to do something about that but in the meantime he got his bag out and told Jack to jump in and be quiet.

He sucked his bottom lip and calmed down and found he was still hungry. He needed something to *eat*. He went looking in the bins. He dug down tentatively into the free papers. Didn't want to catch AIDS. Some of the stuff was all right if it wasn't too far down – from the night before – clean and all that, because he didn't just eat *anything*, wasn't a bin boy. He found a milkshake. He sipped on it but spat it out, twisted his face to get away from the taste because it was strawberry.

"You hungry, boy?" He turned round, instinctively backing away from the voice. A man from an eating place was talking to him. He was skinny and dark and talked funny and was wearing an apron thing like a girl.

"Wait. Stay there and I get you something *hot*." The man walked back into his eating shop. *Pâtisserie* it said. Bully watched him carefully. The man came back out with some cakes and a paper cup.

"From yesterday. But I warm them up, so it's still pretty good."

Bully bit into one hesitantly. It was crumbly like a pasty with chocolate inside. He'd had them before. The man saw the bag move. "What you got in there?"

"Me dog." The man peered into the bag and frowned like he didn't believe him and then stepped back.

"What's that dog doing in there?"

"Restin'," he said, and because Jack was being quiet and

good he fed her one of the little pasties as a reward, even though chocolate was bad for dogs.

Bully took the drink, sipped it, poked his tongue out. Coffee.

"You want sugar?" Bully nodded. "What do you think this is, a café?" The man laughed and gave him three packets out of his apron and Bully emptied them into his cup and threw them away.

"Heh, mind my pavement!"

"What?"

The man pointed to one of the empty sugar packets floating about. Bully put his foot on it.

"You going to pick it up?"

They looked at each other for a few seconds and then the man looked at the bag.

"You want tea instead?"

"Yeah, yeah," said Bully.

"OK… You pick up the paper and I make you tea. Deal?"

Bully nodded but when the man went back inside, he took his foot off the packet and kicked it with his toe into the gutter.

Swish, swish, swish… He heard Jack's Monkey Dog tail wagging inside the bag. She was smelling something … someone. All human beings smelled different to dogs. It was like a fingerprint – no two were the same – and Jack knew everyone Bully knew but by their smell more than anything, more than what they looked like. If the wind was in the right direction, Jack even knew who was coming before they showed up. And sometimes Bully could even tell *who* it was from just how many of those fangy little teeth were showing, because just like any human being, Jack liked some people more than others. A few moments later he saw Stan, wearing a big white shirt and work black trousers, crossing the road, coming to see *him*, chancing it between two cars.

"This … is good…" Stan was standing by the kerb drinking Bully's coffee quickly like it was water. Bully gave Stan the last chocolate pasty. The man from the eating place was standing just inside his shop with the tea in his hand, watching them.

"Nice. Perfect after crash," Stan said. He'd spent the night in a hostel. "Don't like it, you know – all the questions, you know? You got this? You got that? Where you sleep every day – I just say: this is sleeping place? I want to *sleep*, OK. You know?"

"Yeah … yeah. Mick's not around, is he?"

Bully wanted to make sure of this because he wanted to ask Stan for the favour on his own.

"No … still kipping… Bin kipping. You know Mick. No drinking in hostel. So he loves bin. I'm going to bin now and getting him up. You coming?"

"Stan… I won it." He blurted it out, couldn't help it. But Stan was all right. He was on his list.

"What?"

"I got the numbers. I got all of them. I won it!"

"Won what? What you win?"

"The lottery."

"What numbers? What?"

"Camelot… You know." Bully saw the knights in his head, charging around the castle on their dirt bikes, revving up, annoying the neighbours, making bets as to what day in the next five days he was going to turn up.

"What, *this* week? No. I not see you on TV."

"No, it was in February. But, look, there's only five days left on it and you gotta be sixteen before they give it to you, to get the money. So can you do me a favour, yeah? I'll split it with you," he said, without thinking exactly what splitting meant.

Stan rubbed his face and head thoroughly like he was washing it.

"How much? How much you winning?"

"A lot … the lot, you know? *All* of it. But you've got to have something to show them who you are, to prove it, yeah? You got that?"

It didn't say this on the back of the ticket but Bully was now sure of it. Of course they would if it was millions they were handing over. You wouldn't just give millions away without proof, would you? You'd keep it. He didn't believe any of it would be going to charity if he didn't get his claim in. That was just a story. The guy in charge of Camelot would keep it for himself.

"Be fine, be fine…" Stan started walking again. Bully followed him, a little less sure with each step that he'd done the right thing.

"Stan. You got to prove it. Yeah? They *check*, you know. You got a passport?"

That word stopped him, knocked him back on his heels. "Look. I got no papers," he said quickly, to the ground. "OK? I got no *proof*. You need proof, yeah? I got no proof of me. Nothing. Everything in my country at home."

Bully didn't ask where that was because Stan was an illegal. Bully couldn't remember where he came from, even though he'd told him a couple of times. It was one of those long names. Somewhere *Stan*.

"So how much you won?"

"I dunno. The lot."

"About, about how much?"

"Millions." It was always millions.

"Wow." Stan wiped his forehead then got close, put his hand on his shoulder to show he was being serious. "Yeah, you no kidding me?"

Bully shook his head. "No, straight up. No joking," he said.

"So … no one know *you* got the ticket? Yeah?"

"Well, yeah. No … no one knows." There was a long pause. He looked at Stan, saw him working things out, doing his own sums, his hand getting heavier. Then he took it away and smiled.

"So no problem! We get Mick to collect money!"

"Yeah … yeah." Bully didn't like this idea, not one *bite* of it.

"Good, OK. Let's go getting him up!"

"You go."

"No, no, no. We all go!" Stan patted his shoulder, nodded

the way. "Come on. You want your money? Yeah? We not far!" Stan sped off and Bully followed along behind, starting to sweat after a few minutes, with Jack's weight in the bag. He hung back as Stan crossed Shaftesbury Avenue. Stan looked round and waved him across, then when Bully didn't move, came back for him.

"What you doing? Why you so slow?" Bully didn't tell him that he didn't like going out of his territory, because he knew it was stupid. So he looked down, just put one foot in front of the other and followed himself across the road. Still, though, he hung back, didn't like being rushed into new places. And every so often Stan would stop and hurry him along. It felt weird, shops and buildings all a little bit different to the ones he'd got to know since he'd left the flat.

They were nearly there by the time he started thinking about what he would have to give Mick. Was he going to have to give him half of his half or half of Stan's half? Or half for everyone? What were three halves? He had never liked fractions, the way the top numbers were always sitting on the bottom ones, all up themselves, and he was stuck on this sum – resenting the maths he was having to do – when he saw the blue lights reflected in the shop window. There were no sirens and the lights were moving slowly. Bully tapped Stan and they both looked away, Bully putting his hat on, pulling it down round his ears.

"Police men," Stan said, splitting the word up so they sounded like what they were. He never said *Feds*. They waited for the car to go further down the road but it turned the corner into an alleyway, similar to the one Bully bedded down in but much larger, with six or seven eating places backing onto it. In the road was an ambulance and in front of it a big bin truck. One of the grey metal bins was on the back of the truck, two metal arms holding it up in the air. The truck was still making a groaning noise but nothing was moving except the shadow underneath, spreading out into the alleyway.

Stan was in the bin on the back of the truck before the policemen were even out of their car. Black bags came flying out, popping on the warm tarmac. Stan was screaming and shouting all sorts but the only word Bully could make out was *Mick*. All the rest of it was from somewhere else.

He didn't wait around.

"We got to go back," he said to Jack, because there was no one else left anywhere near the top of his list and now he would have to go searching much, much further down...

5

04 **11** **10**
DAYS HOURS MINUTES

Win big! Win tonight! it said in yellow letters as big as Bully on the giant screen above the zombies at Waterloo.

He waited until one of the guards opened up the disabled gates for a woman with a pram and followed her onto the platform.

"Mum ... Mum," he said, making her look round, making the guard think they were on the same family ticket, him carrying the bags.

He got on the train and hid in the toilets until the guard went past. He didn't have to stay there long. It was only five stops between the flat and his doorway off Old Paradise Street.

When the train arrived at the station Bully went over the railing and into the car park, Jack on his back in the holdall. He landed on his feet, on the bonnet of a Fiesta. For the fun of it he ran across three cars to get to the exit. Someone shouted "Oi!" but no one did anything.

The flat was less than a Scooby-Doo away from the station. Twenty minutes max. Before he'd learned to read a clock he used to measure out the day in Scoobies because it was his favourite cartoon when he was little and watched cartoons. His old life slowed him down on the way back to the flat, though. It kept jumping out at him, and everything seemed too close, as if he'd put his glasses back on, and it took him a whole Scooby-Doo and a half just to get back to where he'd left the ashes in the bit of dirt.

It didn't look the same. The broken stone he'd left to mark the spot was covered over with stringy, straggly orange and yellow weeds, just squatting there. He poked around with a stick to clear a patch and then paid his respects, made sure Jack didn't wee anywhere and made his mind up to come back another day.

He nearly went to the wrong block. All the blocks were in a line and each block on the estate had a big huge arch in it, so that from far away it looked like a giant rat had gnawed its way through all of them. They'd only moved into the new flat overlooking the road tunnelling underneath just before his mum started getting ill. They'd done an exchange and got one with three bedrooms so he didn't have to share with his half-sister Cortnie any more. Though now his mum was dead, he didn't consider any fraction of Cortnie as relating much to him at all.

A few people on the estate stared like they thought they recognized this boy in the hot green coat on a summer's day but no one said his name out loud.

He took the stairs instead of chancing the lift. His old flat was fifteen flats from the lift doors, eleven from the stairs, and just one down from the rubbish chute. He was pretty sure it was why the old man who used to live in it had wanted to swap. No one liked having a chute clanging and banging at all hours, even though the sign on it said to be considerate to your neighbours. He pulled it open to see if there was anything he could eat jammed in the top, like a pizza box, but it was empty. There was just the smell of all that old waste still hanging on to the dark.

He could hear the little kid Declan next door, crying up against the letter box, wanting to play out. He wasn't allowed to unless his brother was with him because it was too dangerous with the stairs. The little kids played with the rubbish chute, sticking toys and stuff down it, and maybe falling down it, and Bully had looked after his own sister too when he used to live here.

"All right, Declan," he said, and Declan stopped crying for a sec and then started up again.

Outside his flat Bully flapped the letter box, looking up and down the concrete landing, his heart going and him just standing there not going nowhere.

No one was in. He had a look-see through. In the hall was a *cat*. It was psycho, staring right back at him, just like cats did. He wondered what it was doing there. Phil didn't like dogs or cats or anything else with more legs than him. It was another reason why Bully had left. He still had his mum's set of keys and he let himself in. Jack barked at the cat and it ran into Phil's bedroom and then Bully thought maybe it was *her* cat.

The smell of the empty fryer set his stomach going.

He could taste the fat in the air. Another smell too, paint coming from somewhere. He went through to the kitchen. It looked different from when he left; his mum's spider plant was missing from the top of the fridge and two of the kitchen walls had been done up purple. A dirty paintbrush was still on the side of the sink, its roots sky-blue.

First thing he did was feel the kettle. No heat there, not even smack warm, the plastic colder than he was. Phil always had a brew on the go and Bully was an expert at judging how long boiled water took to cool down to nothing. And Bully was pretty sure Phil had left the flat before the middle of the day. He would either be back soon or not for a while yet. If Phil was out for longer than a few hours, he was gone all day. It was the way he worked.

Bully put a bowl of water out for Jack and was going to defrost some mince when he saw tins of cat food stacked up against the fridge. He picked one up and, hiding it from Jack, he took out the empty tin he'd saved from yesterday and put some of it in that.

"It's for dogs," he said, serving it up but keeping the can. Then he went looking for his own meal. In the cupboards he found a packet of Rich Tea biscuits and a family bag of crisps and got some bread and margarine and made himself a crisp sandwich. There was half a bottle of Coke in the fridge and he had that. It was flat but that didn't bother him. He could drink flat Coke like it was water.

He stayed in the kitchen, eating and listening out for the front door. There was a letter from his school, unopened, on the side. Bully picked it up, examined it. He knew what that was about – bet Phil had had a few of those in the last few months. He threw it in the bin and then went back into the hall to put his phone on charge because that was where his mum always used to do it. On top of the meter were two tens for the electric, his old square glasses weighing them down. He tried them on; the insides of the flat were suddenly too close, just like the outsides had been, walking from the station. And he took them off but put them in his coat pocket.

He left the money where it was and went into the lounge. The curtains were still drawn and it was the same as he remembered, just cleaner looking. The TV was new though. He felt tired, very tired, and lay down on the old couch. The new cushions on it were bright and scratchy. He flung them at the end and spent a few minutes working out the TV. He used to sleep here like this when his mum was dying. He used to like drifting off to the voices on the TV, still in the room with him whether he was awake or not.

He flicked through the channels without interest and then he fell asleep.

04 **06** **52**
DAYS HOURS MINUTES

A scream went off somewhere just outside Bully's head. His eyes popped and a little girl with long hair was staring at him. She looked a lot like his half-sister except this one had dolly-cut hair and a bigger, redder face.

"Dad! BRADLEY'S BACK! It's Bradley!" she said. Then she screamed again when she saw Jack coming out from underneath the cushions, as if she'd never seen her before.

"Cortnie! Shut it!" Phil was there in the room now. He was worse than Bully for noises. He couldn't put up with any of them any more.

"You back then?" he said, looking at Jack.

"It's all right. I'm not stayin'." His mouth felt sticky and dry from the Coke and biscuits.

He expected Phil to lose it, go off on one, but all he said was, "Suit yourself."

He tried to work out how long he'd been asleep. The TV was still on. News and quizzes and stuff. Must be getting on.

"You want tea or what?" Without waiting for an answer, Phil went into the kitchen.

"You stayin', Bradley?" Cortnie asked, getting a little braver and sidling up to him. It felt like it had been a long time since anyone had called him that. It was strange hearing this other name as if he was watching the news about himself, about this Bradley boy who'd gone back to where he used to live with his mum and half a sister.

"Shut up," he said.

She tried another tack. "We been out, Bradley… Bet you don't know where we been? We've been to see *Em-ma*," she said, speaking like a dolly did.

"*She* not here then?" he said sarcastically. He refused to use her name. "Is that *her* cat?"

"No. She's *mine*, Bradley."

He was flabbergasted by that. "That's *your* cat? Who got *you* a cat?"

"Daddy did."

Bully winced. He'd had to put up with the *D* word since Cortnie was born but he hadn't heard it for a while now.

"Yeah, so it's all right for you, is it? To have *cats*?"

She looked confused. She didn't understand why he was so angry.

"She's called Chloe. And we got the *best* one from the … litter," she said, remembering the right word but thinking it might be wrong because it meant rubbish too. "We've been … to see Emma – and we got a takeout to celebrate… D'you know where we've been then, Bradley? We been to see Emma and someone *special*, Bradley… Bradley…" She shook his arm. "You're not listenin'."

He wished she would stop calling him that. But this was good news. Maybe *she* wasn't living here after all. She was supposed to be moving in the day he moved out. Phil had been seeing her on the side, he knew that. He'd been smelling the scent of someone else on Phil's clothes months before his mum died. And before *she* was even in the flat she'd worked Phil up to getting rid of his mum's stuff: her clothes, her shoes, her knick-knacks; all down the chute into the bins, along with the rest of her.

"*Here.*" Phil handed him his tea and Bully tasted it, then took a mouthful, a big rinser. It was how he liked it: not too hot and sweet. He heard himself mumbling, "Cheers."

"Porr! You *stink*. Off that couch now and get and have a wash."

Bully didn't take it personally, it wasn't something that bothered him, but he denied it all the same.

"I won't say it again," said Phil. And Bully knew he wouldn't, so he went. "And take that dog with you," Phil added as Jack followed him into the hall.

In the bathroom Bully ran the hot tap. He sat on the edge of the bath, watching the water creep up the side. He took his coat and top off and shoes and socks. The last time he'd got undressed was at Waterloo where he'd had a wash in the toilets, *in* the toilet for a bit of privacy – didn't want to show his bits, did he? Flushed it first of course.

Jack was up at the door, trying to get at the cat. It reminded Bully of Declan wanting to play out. Phil shouted something about paintwork from the lounge.

"Stop scratching!" said Bully. He still had his mug of tea with him and every few sips he dipped his toes into the water, testing the temperature like he was thinking about going for a paddle but not for a swim. It was too boiling hot. His mum always ran the cold first – to be on the safe side, she said. But it was a long time since she'd run him a bath. He turned the cold tap on and knocked some tubes of make-up into the water. *Her* stuff.

"You in there?" Phil opened the door as he asked the question and Bully held his coat up to cover his top half.

He pointed at Bully's hair. "*That* needs cutting. And *they* want binning," he said, pointing at his jeans. "I'll hook you out a pair of mine for now." Bully didn't ask where his stuff was. He could guess.

"What's all that doin' in there?" Phil's voice hardened. He was looking at the make-up in the bath, the tubes bobbling about under the taps.

"Fell in…"

"Well, it'd better fall out then." He expected Phil to go for him but he was just staring, still measuring him up. "You got taller?"

Bully nodded.

"Phil…" he said, though he hadn't used his name for … *years.*

"Yeah, what?"

"You ever got lucky? You know, like, *lucky* lucky?"

"Took one for my country," he said, looking down at his chest where the bullet had gone in. "That lucky, was it? Why? What you done? What you been up to?"

"Nothin'."

Phil looked him up and down as if he was inspecting him, like in the army. "You had any trouble? Turn round," he said and he looked Bully over until he was satisfied there was no sign of any visible wounds.

Jack started growling. "I'm all right, mate," Bully said to his dog and put his coat back on.

"If that thing goes for me," said Phil.

"I'm not stayin'."

"So what you doing here for, then? What's up? What's going down?"

"Nothing. Just … came back… That's all." He paused for Phil to ask him where he'd come back from, what he'd been living off, but all he said was, "So you stayin' for any of this takeout or what?" Bully shook his head then nodded. "Right, get and have that bath then. And clean this lot up. And while you're here, keep that dog out of my way…"

Phil went into the hall and then turned back with his hand still on the door. "I know she's not your mum, but Emma's all right. She was worried about you, you know? I told her you were staying with my dad until we got settled. So you don't say anything when you see 'er, right? She's coming back tomorrow. Cortnie told you, did she?"

Bully nodded, looked down, showed his disappointment to the carpeted floor. So she had moved in then. Where was she? Out shopping, wasting money, he expected. On *clothes*.

"It's been hard for us all, Bradley, all *this*… Not just you, you know – me and your sister as well. I know you were close to your mum but life goes on," Phil said. "You can stay if you like but that thing'll have to go sooner or later. You can't have a dog like that around little ones."

Bully said nothing, just waited for the door to close again. He didn't feel anything when Phil had spoken about his mum. He thought he would get angry with him but there was nothing there. He didn't understand it.

He didn't get in the bath but sat on the side, thinking about whether he could trust Phil enough to tell him about the ticket before *she* got back. He didn't particularly care about Phil saying Jack had to go sooner or later. It wasn't in his plans to come back to the flat for good anyway. Now he could get his own place, with his own money, what did he need a crappy little flat for? But maybe he could stay tonight and see how it went and maybe tell Phil about his ticket when Cortnie went to bed. He still hated him for the bad thing that he'd done, but he might still be good for something.

He put his hand into the water and splashed it about. It was nearly right, nearly time to get in, and he looked around the bathroom for a towel. There weren't any. He wouldn't bother normally, just drip dry, but there was no lock on the door. He didn't want Cortnie coming in and doing more screaming.

"Stay, stay…" he said to Jack and went to see if they still kept towels in the airing cupboard. Along the hall the smell of the paint became stronger. He looked in on Cortnie's room. It was still pink but the posters were different on the walls, pop stars now instead of made-up things. He picked out a towel from the airing cupboard, one he remembered with the face of a washed-out train running through it. He walked along to his bedroom because that was where the smell was coming from. The door was shut. As he opened it he thought about why the roots of the paintbrush were blue.

The colour hit him like a back-hander. Everything was sky-blue, except for the ceiling. And there were pictures of cars and trains running around the top, and his bed was gone and in its place was a tiny, tiny white cot.

She was having a baby. She'd *had* the baby … *someone special*. And from the colour on the four walls surrounding him he could see *it* was a baby boy.

He went back to the bathroom. He put his clothes and trainers on and tiptoed to the front door with Jack whining, knowing something was up. He unplugged his mobile, took one of the tenners off the electric meter and just before he let himself out, he felt for his glasses in his pocket and threw them on the floor.

And back through the hallway he could still hear the cold tap running.

04 **02** **45**
DAYS HOURS MINUTES

He could not trust Phil. He should have known he was way too far down his list. If he gave the ticket to Phil, he wouldn't get his money back. *He* would waste it all on *her*, and *it*, the new boy.

There was no one left in his family now. Cortnie didn't count. It was just him and Jack.

Less than a Scooby-Doo later, he was back on the next train to London. There was no guard and he sat with his feet on the seat, Jack there too, waiting for someone to say something. He could tell they wanted to but nobody did, not with Jack beside him, showing her shiny little teeth. And he liked that feeling of upsetting the passengers around him, knowing they were thinking about him, that they couldn't ignore him. It made him feel better for a while.

It was nearly dark when the train began to slow down, looking for its platform, and he could see the lights squaring up the houses that ran along the track. He got straight off when the doors opened. He didn't look for anyone to go through the gate with, just forced his way through the automatic ticket barrier, Jack slipping underneath.

He bought three burgers and loped around the station, feeding bits of them to Jack. He spent his time adding up how many hours he had left to claim: four days = 24 x 4 + 1½ left from tonight = around 100. He didn't give it an exact number in case it was less.

With the last of his big money he bought a sausage roll that left him with nothing to top up his phone, just shrapnel.

He turned it on anyway. He got a message. Before he could open it, he got another and another and another … and another. They kept coming.

Phone or text me now! Riz xxxxxxxxx

He didn't know any Riz but the name and the kisses made it sound like a girl.

Lend us a grand! Real deal for operation for me nan u no? Chaz.

No, he didn't know *Chaz* or her nan.

The two Sammies must have passed his number round. And he hated them now, especially the other Sammy because she said mushy things about wanting to be his mum.

He read the rest of them: begging, pleading and even threatening him for money he didn't have. Then his phone started ringing – numbers he didn't know. He looked around as if it might be someone in the station – then he hit the red button and turned his phone off. He weaved through the late-night zombies and headed for the train drivers' steps, changed his mind and left the station by the taxi-rank entrance.

He walked round the back of the building, past the end of Old Paradise Road, the dancing lady on the brick wall laughing her head off at him; at how stupid he'd been to think that he could trust Phil.

He kept licking his lips. He was thirsty from the burgers and tired, his feet dragging, his trainers paper thin at the toes. But in less than five minutes he would be dossing down in his usual spot. And tomorrow he would have to make a move and start heading for Camelot. His thinking now was that he would find someone on the way to help him, someone like the nice lady who gave him twenty quid. It was a pity he couldn't find her again, he thought. But that was the problem with people who weren't on the streets; you didn't know where they lived.

Before he got to his place it started raining, and he went to McDonald's to get a drink. He put Jack in her bag and struck lucky on the first table by the door: a hot chocolate, still warm. He picked up some sugars and took it downstairs to the toilets because he needed to wee. He filled his water bottle. The plastic crackled as he forced it to fit under the tap. His head and heart were calmer now he was back on his territory but his legs were heavy as if all that anger and upset had melted right down inside them. He couldn't face even walking back up the stairs, let alone outside in the rain to get to his alleyway. He would take a short cut.

He went out into the corridor, past the crew room to the emergency exit and put Jack on her feet. The alarm would go off when he opened the door but the manager would just think it was rubbish being dumped. He pushed on the metal bar to break the fire door open and the alarm rang the way it always did, though louder right in his ears.

He looked out at his alleyway. He could see his step settling in the shadows. The rain touched his face. He pictured himself cozying up dry and warm in his sleeping bag, watching the weather drip and blow. Something, though, was different about his doorway. Perhaps it was just strange to see it from this angle, but it was like one of those stupid kids' magazines where they had two pictures that were exactly the same, except for *one* thing. And you had to spot what it was to win a stupid prize. And he puzzled over it for a moment, the alarm still going, and then he got it, what was different about *this* picture compared to the one he'd left this morning. His wheelie bin was facing the wrong way.

He was still staring at his bin, wondering about it, when the green lid crept up a couple of centimetres. Something inside was trying to get out! There … a strip of brown fur! A rat! Getting at his stuff!

He moved out into the alleyway to find something to hit it with but then he looked again, his mouth opening up because what he was seeing wasn't fur, it was *hair*.

The shock of it wiped his mind clean away. The lid flipped back on its hinges and he watched a joke of a man struggling to get out of the bin, whilst jabbing and pointing at him.

Still Bully couldn't move. He had to reboot and that took a few seconds. And like most people caught up in a *situation*, he didn't have much more than a few seconds…

"Give us a hand!" the man was shouting. And Bully saw two men peel away from the walls at the entrance to the alleyway and come running.

Crash! The bin toppled over. The man inside groaned and swore for help but Bully knew they weren't running to help him, they weren't helping anybody but themselves. He didn't know who they were. He didn't recognize them but he instinctively knew they were that breed of men that would take what they wanted from him, without begging for it. And they wanted his *ticket*.

And now he was back online, his system up and running, and he stumbled inside. He grabbed the bar of the fire door to slam it in their faces.

But where was Jack?

"Here! Jacky! Jacky!" he said in a hard whisper like he might still hide from these men. And then he yelled it, louder, in case she thought it was a game.

Bully forced himself to look up, to gauge the distance left between them and him. The men were still the other side of the bins but no more than a long spit away from the door, and he frantically slapped his knees like Jack was a puppy. And there she was! Belly on the tarmac coming out from *under* the bin with a rat between her fangy teeth.

"Here, girl!" he yelled, pulling on the metal bar of the door. And he snatched a last look at the men he'd never seen before, sharpening up in the shadows without him having to squint, getting bigger, much bigger than him, with Jack *just* coming through the door ahead of them.

"Come on, girl, come on!" And Jack knew it was no game they were playing and she was through the gap and Bully was pulling as hard as he could with both hands on that metal bar.

The split second before the fire door locked, a body on the other side ran into it – *bam!* – doing the job for him. And then Bully was taking the stairs two at time, a different boy to the one with shot legs a few minutes ago. And he flew past a burger boy, back the way he'd come, dirty looks swelling up with horror on all the eating faces because Jack still had that rat in her mouth.

Outside he ran blind, straight across Old Paradise Road without looking, heard the car braking afterwards, voices shouting, then in the distance his name chasing after him. *"Bully..."*

At the main road on the way to the river he looked down into the mouth of the old tunnel. He could lose them if he went down there and they ran on, thinking he'd crossed over, making straight for the river.

He hesitated then took a chance, went down the concrete slip, skidding, his legs nearly overtaking him like he was running away from a smack. He ran as hard as he could, keeping away from the strip lighting, the graffiti bubbling away on the walls. Back on the estate he'd had his own tag: a *B* with a squiggle on the end. The *B* had been for Bradley then. What the squiggle was for he never really knew.

Up ahead a bright flash, then another, stopped him for a second: what was *that*? A torch? A bike? No sound to it, just *light*. And then behind him he heard a man shout. He looked round and saw two shadows slipping along the walls, the echo of their feet already catching up with him; they had followed him down.

03 **23** **50**
DAYS HOURS MINUTES

He swore at himself for getting things wrong again. He was always doing that at school and getting caught out.

He saw faces in the flashes of light up ahead. And he ran towards them. There were people inside the tunnel taking photos on their phones, just standing still, waiting … queuing, that's what they were doing. He saw the sign then, glowing red, set into the wall. @ it said. And there was a door! Two men in black and white were guarding it, one tall, one small, and both as wide as each other. Bully ran straight in behind the taller one. He didn't see Bully until he was almost through the door, didn't make a move until the last second, but when he did it was quick and his hand shot out and grabbed Bully's shoulder. The big guy's fingers jabbed into his collarbone but couldn't grip the greasy coat and Bully was away. Not for one single second did it occur to him to stop and ask either man for help.

"Look! There's a boy!" People laughed and then "Oh! What the – what is that *thing*!" they gasped when they saw the funny-looking dog galloping at his feet. Bully kept going, in between the red and black tables, across the dance floor, knocking women off their heels, one, two, three ... and into the kitchens: staff in their whites freeze-framing in the bright light, too slow to stop him because he knew *where* he was going now – full pelt towards the little green man on the exit sign, already off and running...

He came out underneath a railway arch. He hid behind one of the cars parked in the street, catching his breath, watching the door to the kitchens to see what came out of it.

Through the car windows he saw both of the bouncers having a look round and then going back inside. A taxi went past, rumbling on the stones. He was near the river, but he had to cross it to go north to Watford to get to Camelot. He couldn't face that journey *now*, not tonight, not in the dark, with those men behind him, catching up with him out in the open, running across the bridge. So he headed away from the river, looking for somewhere out of the rain, somewhere safe to last the night. But away from the river, every road they went down was just another he didn't recognize, rows of houses crowding in, all looking the same, TVs warm and bright with advertisements. He thought about knocking on a door but what would they do? See him off or call the police. And then where would he be? Stuck answering questions, all his chances of winning *lost*.

The rain started to hit hard, like it was trying to make him wet, staining his jeans a new temporary dark blue. He looked down at Jack, with her waterproof fur. Rain never got her *soaking* wet. He poked his head as far down into his jacket as he could get it, and when he next took a look he was on *Kennington Road*. And there across the road, on the other side of the railings, was a big white house lit up inside a park. What drew him to it were two big, big guns, as big as buses, parked side by side on the lawn, pointing towards the river. Any place with guns was a safe place. And maybe he could hide out round the back of the house in a doorway and go back down to the river tomorrow, and cross further downstream.

He ran to the iron gates. His feet were wet and sore. No one was around, just cars swishing up and down the road through the rain. He shoved Jack inside his coat and climbed up, jamming his toes in the gaps in the ironwork.

When he got to the top it looked as if the ground had shrunk. He hesitated then began to climb down the other side. He slipped – no grip – and the leg of his jeans caught on a spike, leaving him hanging there upside down, Jack scrabbling with her paws and scratching his face. He swore, unhooked himself and dropped.

He got up, hopping and swearing. *"Jesus wet, Jesus wet,"* he said, because he'd twisted his ankle and his mum used to say it when things got twisted. And it *was* raining and he *was* soaking wet just like Jesus.

He looked around the park. There was no moon and away from the streetlights the ground quickly went black until it met the light from the big white house. He made for a small clump of trees next to the house, limping still. It was drier under the branches for a while but then he felt the rain beginning to work its way down through the gaps in the leaves and he ran over to the pointy porch at the front of the house. He read the sign above the glass doors.

IMP...ER...IAL WAR MUS...EUM

He'd been to a museum once. Trips at school were free if you were poor, but after the first couple, he'd started losing the teachers' letters.

He had a good look now, through the glass doors, for free. Inside the museum, hanging down from the ceiling on wires, was an old plane that looked like it had been stuck together from bits and pieces off the street. The tank underneath it looked real though, made of metal and bashed about like it had been in a proper war. And there was a rocket too, the top bit with the men in it that came back down to earth, like the end of a giant blunt pencil.

Bully shook the glass doors. They were too thick to break and though it was dry here under the porch, he didn't feel safe in the light, so he went to hide out of sight under the artillery guns sticking out of the lawn.

He crouched down by the breach where the shells went in and where it was dry. Jack started licking at his shins. His twisted ankle felt numb now. He looked at the other one with his lighter. There was blood on one of his trainers, leaking out of him somewhere. He let Jack lick it off until he remembered the rat that had been in her mouth, then he pulled his foot away.

He examined the round breach above his head, much bigger than his head. These were big, big guns. Pity they were pointing north instead of south. He could knock out his old flat easy from here, even though it was six or seven miles away, take out the whole block – Phil and *her* and *it* – with just a couple of shells. Because each gun took a shell that was as big as a grown man, each barrel was maybe 15 to 20 inches across … *the calibre*, that's what it was called. And old guns were measured in inches and new guns were measured in millimetres. Phil had taught him that; the sizes and proper names for things that killed you. And big guns were called howitzers and cannons, and fired shells, but little guns fired bullets and they were called rounds. And bombs were IEDs. And anything coming *at* you was *incoming...* And you'd better duck, otherwise you were—

He suddenly panicked that his ticket was getting wet and unzipped the little pocket inside his jacket and took it out. It was still in one piece but the top of it was damp. He cried out when it tore a little. He needed a better, safer place to hide it. His hoodie didn't have a zip pocket and his jeans were wet.

He hooked out the family bag of crisps he'd taken from the flat and finished them off. Then he turned the packet foil-side out, cut a patch out of it and wrapped the ticket up. That would keep it dry but where was he going to hide it? He didn't fancy stuffing it up his bum like they did in prison. He couldn't see how that worked anyway because what happened when you had to *go*? What about if he shoved it in his ear hole? But he didn't like things in his ears. He'd had a beetle in there once when he was little and no one believed him until it uncurled itself the next day and flew out. He didn't have any big holes in his teeth to jam it in, they were all filled. And it was no good poking it up his nose either because he had a cold and it was runny. He was always picking it anyway.

While he had a think, he let Jack crawl inside his coat like it was a tent. He rubbed her head and her dog tag jingle-jangled. It was a shame it was just solid metal and didn't open up like some of his mum's jewellery did. He felt round her collar. It had been getting tight, pinching her because it was for a puppy, until Bully cut another notch in it. He took it off and had a closer look at it with his lighter. It was basically two strips of leather sewn together. He got his penknife out and started unpicking the stitching with the shorter blade. It was a tricky job. He kept missing the stitches and burning his fingers on the lighter – and the stitches were so tiny, like cutting up fleas, but he managed to work the blade in between the leather and open up a gap.

He folded the crisp packet up until it was about the size of the end of his little fingernail and prodded it in with his metal spoon. He couldn't sew it together but he always had gum on him and he chewed up an old piece and stoppered the hole. Once that stuff set, it was like concrete. He'd seen the men in high-vis blasting it off the pavements on the Strand.

He put Jack's collar back on. Her fur was nearly the same colour as the collar. He rubbed a bit of dirt and grease from his coat into the chewing-gum to make it look more like the leather. Jack licked his face.

"You're a million-dollar dog now," he said, stroking her head. And then in the darkness he felt her ears go back, like she was a *bat* dog.

He flicked his lighter on to see what she was thinking. She was listening to something... Something Bully couldn't hear yet but when he saw her eyes go very still, he knew what it was.

03 23 01
DAYS HOURS MINUTES

It was the sound of a dog, after them, following the invisible trail they had laid. Someone must have taken his bedding as scent for their dog. And a trained dog could follow their scent, chase their smell all round London for at least a day.

And Jack knew it too. And she was telling Bully now, showing her cleverness the only way she knew how, growling and whining, asking Bully: *Do we fight or run away?* Because someone was coming for them, coming for his millions with a dog, and from the way Jack's eyes were beading up she knew *which* dog, too. Bully caught sight of the notch torn out of her ear: Janks. Janks was *here*, looking to tax Bully of everything he had.

Jack snapped at the darkness. And this time Bully just about heard the tail end of a howl. It was coming, he thought, from behind the back of the house, another gate on the other side of the park. He licked his first finger and held it up to the air... Not much wind but maybe enough to take their scent in the *wrong* direction. He didn't think he could outrun them now, not with his ankle this bad.

He scanned the park. *Never get caught on open ground…* All he could see were black blobs, litter bins dotted about – he could maybe just about fit in one, doubled up with Jack, pull some rubbish over their heads. Instinctively, though, he knew they needed to find *higher ground*.

He ran to the trees. He tried to jump up to reach the lowest branch. He didn't miss it by much but when he landed his ankle collapsed under him and he knew it wouldn't take another fall. He tried climbing then, wrapping his arms around the trunk, but his foot kept letting him down. Even if he got up the tree and dragged Jack up … *even* if they got up the tree, the dog would find them, because any old dog would know they were up there. Even if they went right to the top, Janks's dog would see him in between the branches and the leaves, no matter how dark it was.

That thought gave him half an idea. He took his coat off. He fumbled about with numb fingers and got his phone out, and his penknife and Jack's lead. He tied the lead around his neck because his pockets were too small. He heard another howl, the sound getting closer. He panicked and threw his coat up into the branches as high as he could with whatever else was left in his pockets. And as it left his hand he felt a small emptiness open up inside his head that told him he'd forgotten something… His card! His *mum's* card. He tried jumping up to get it back but it was too late. He smacked the back of his neck. How stupid he was! But he had to go now. And he took off his trainers and balled up his socks and threw them back towards the war museum, and then his phone too because the screen was smashed in and leaking grey and black. No good to him any more. He threw all his stuff as far away as he could, like a *false* trail. That might mess things up for a while. The rain might be thinning out his real tracks, he thought, as he limped back to the guns to crouch underneath them.

He knew that hiding under the guns was a bad place to be but he didn't know where else to go. He couldn't think, couldn't get the dots to join up inside his head. The sharper sound of the dog barking snapped Bully's head back into the steel breach – the dog somewhere inside the park now – his last line of defence gone.

Panic is a killer … takes your head off as neat as a round…

"Come on…" he said, slapping his ears. *"Come on…"*

Then he got the other half of his idea.

He got out from underneath the guns and stood up. He could just about see the outline of the two barrels tapering off into the darkness. If he could climb up there and go right to the end of the barrel, then even if he couldn't get away, it was at least a position he could *defend*.

The first thing he did was stash Jack inside his hoodie, tucking his top in like his mum used to do to him when he was little. "Stay," he said, clambering up onto the gun, struggling with Jack's weight on his front – like carrying a four-legged baby.

The angle of elevation was steeper than it looked from the

ground but he managed to stand up on the barrel. The metal was cold under his feet, and his ankle started to hurt again without his shoes. It wasn't as wide as he'd thought and he had to sidestep, balancing with his arms like he was one of those street performers messing about for money.

He'd been higher up than this before; much, much higher, on the roof of their old block of flats. He'd gone up there one day to see what it was like looking all that way down without anything to hold on to. He wasn't frightened then, not in the way he was now, in the dark, in the rain, where looking down was all around him. He tried not to look down, but couldn't help it. The ground kept tugging at his head. And when he did, he slipped and fell.

He threw his arms wide and caught the barrel but hit his jaw against Jack's skull and she snapped at him, caught him on the ear. But Bully didn't care for a few long seconds. And he put his face to the metal and hugged it almost harder than he'd hugged anything or anyone in his life. And though he was squashing Jack against the barrel, and she was wriggling out onto the gun, he couldn't move, couldn't go any further...

03 **22** **50**
DAYS HOURS MINUTES

Jack got her head out from under his and licked his ear, whimpering, thinking she had done something wrong and this was her punishment, being stuck up here, squashed inside Bully's hoodie.

"All right ... all right..." he whispered. "Shh. Shut it... All right... All right..." He gave his dog some air, let go a little, took his face away from the barrel and she stopped struggling.

He slowly raised his head and then sat up. He could see the lights from the road and the cars and the buildings speckling in the rain. He realized it was no good being up here if Janks found him, no way he could defend himself just sitting on the barrel. He would fall off. There was only one place left to go when he got to the end: *inside* the gun.

He could hear a pit bull clearly now, though he could not risk turning round to look back at the museum. And it *was* a pit bull, he was sure of it; less echo to its bark, more bite, as if that was the only thing going through its head. He pushed forward with his knees, getting into a rhythm, still hugging the barrel until he felt the steel lip of the mouth.

But something was covering the end. It made a plasticky *thwacking* noise, like a sheet of tarpaulin covering the back of a truck, and though he hit it with his fist, there was no give in it. He tried to pull it off but it was tied on with a metal rope looped around the barrel's end. And it was too late to get back down. The barking was louder, *keener*, the dog getting a real taste for his scent now, getting closer and closer. And voices! He could hear men shouting directions. He took out his penknife, opened the big blade up and slashed at the thick plastic two, three times, putting all his effort into pulling the blade through the material.

He went feet first, with Jack's paws round his neck,

clinging on, then scrabbling, trying to get out. Bully couldn't blame her, felt as if he was being swallowed alive himself – and he began to struggle too. And then he was stuck.

He held his breath. Half in, half out of the barrel, he had a split-second horror of the dog getting up here and taking chunks out of him, as easy as ice cream. He frantically twisted sideways, skinning his hips, the widest part of him, but wedging himself tighter in, trying to keep a hold of Jack.

"Calm it! Calm it down," he whispered. But he wasn't calm. He wasn't calming it down. What could he do? He had to be thinner! He had to make himself the *right calibre*. How could he do that? He let go his breath and felt a bit of give in the little bit of fat and skin between his insides and the barrel. And he slipped; he moved just a little… He let out more breath, emptied his lungs, *pushed* out his spare air and shifted one side of his body down at an angle, collapsing it like a cardboard box. And then *right down* he went inside the barrel.

When he got to his shoulders he wondered how he was going to stop them sliding *all* the way down? And he was having to think off the top of his head and to *shh* Jack, and keep himself from slipping down. He tapped Jack on her muzzle, telling her to *cut it out*, and felt the lead still round his neck. And with one hand he pulled it off and opened up the large metal hook on it and jammed it over the metal rope around the rim. And like a climber going into a cave, he lowered himself and Jack right down inside the gun.

Instantly his world went out. He lay there, arms stretched

above his head, blinking in the darkness but seeing nothing. He could hear everything though, even louder inside the barrel: the creaking wet lead, Jack panting ever so quick, and louder than everything, the voice inside his head telling him to get out, to get *out*.

And then a man's voice crept down the barrel, one that he knew, putting the shudders into him, the words seesawing up and down, shouting and giving orders.

"All-right … list-en! *You* check the bins while I have a look round here."

"What's he gunna be doing in a *bin*!"

"Just do what I say," said Janks.

Bully pushed his ear flat against the cold steel of the bore, and against the splatter of the rain he could hear the other voice still complaining, asking questions, and he realized there were just two men.

"Here, Janks! Over 'ere! Here's his coat … and his shoes. And a mobile. He's up that tree!"

But the pit bull whined like it knew better and then the whine deepened into a howl, and Bully thought he could hear it straining at the lead, the scent of the chase thick as soup in its mouth now because it *knew* where they were.

Still, though, Bully begged his plan to work. Maybe when they saw he wasn't up the tree they'd think he'd made a run for it. He twisted a little, shivering on the end of the dog lead because he was encased inside a couple of hundred tonnes of cold steel.

Plink! What was that? *Plink … plink…* His last little bit of shrapnel rolling away. He had a hole in his jeans. Never much money in them to lose. He couldn't get to his pocket; had to lie there like he was tied up and listen... *Plink ... plink ... plink...* And he knew that even in the rain, Janks's dog would be hearing it too.

He kept *very, very* still. Sweat and rain dribbled and mixed down his back. Then he heard a different noise, not metal on metal but a living, skittering, scratching sound ... something coming *up* the barrel! And he thought of all those films he'd seen with aliens and insects hatching out of the darkness. There it was again! He couldn't look down but put his chin to his chest and felt Jack's nose twitch against his neck. And Jack made the quietest bark she had – a little cough – like in class at school, getting a message across without the teacher turning round, and Bully understood what it was then: Janks's dog was *on* the gun.

He got ready with his knife still in his left hand. He waited. The rain was making his grip slip on the lead and he twisted it around his wrist so he could still stab the pit bull's snout with his other hand.

"What's 'e doing up there, Janks?" shouted the other man. He sounded miserable and angry. "What's 'e doing? Look at 'im... Just look at 'im! What's gone *wrong* with 'im!"

The scratching stopped. A yelp, thinning, falling... And the man laughing, mean and hollow. The dog had slipped and hit the ground, that's what it was! The dog had slipped and fallen off the barrel! And the man was laughing at that and making fun of Janks's dog.

"I mean, look at 'im, Janks! Look at 'im… What is this, Janks? A wind-up? I mean, this is turnin' into a *joke*."

"You think I'm a joke?"

"No, Janks… Not *you*, that dog of yours. And all *this*."

"Come here and *say* it then."

"No, come on, Janks. I'm just sayin'…"

For three or four of Bully's breaths it was quiet outside the gun, as if everything had been said. And then he heard the two men begin to threaten each other, grunts and yells bursting out between their words, so that Bully couldn't tell exactly what was happening until he heard a sound that very few men will ever make more than once in their lives.

In and around London, in the first hours of the morning, mobile phones lit up with a screenshot of a boy and his dog. And a message:

Stray on the loose answers to the name of bully last seen on the south bank heading north to watford – big reward offered for safe return JANKS

And a good many men rubbed their eyes and went back to sleep, thinking nothing more about it. But in bright little flats in dark little places, a few paused for a moment in what they were doing (to the relief of some) to seriously consider this offer. And though most of these men went back to doing what they were doing, more than one or two decided they wanted *in* on this. And *all* these men – fat, thin, tall, short and funny-looking – had one thing in common: they didn't *care* what they were searching for. They just wanted the money. And before the sun came up they were buzzing through London, on the lookout for a stray named Bully who was going to make them rich.

03 **20** **35**
DAYS HOURS MINUTES

Bully woke and choked, Jack licking his face, spit and snot going *up* his nose. He strained his neck to lift his eyes and saw a streak of grey painted into the darkness.

In summer the light came back in the middle of the night, a long time before the sun, and he guessed he hadn't been unconscious for more than a couple of hours. He tried to pull himself up on Jack's dog lead but his arms weren't listening to his head, refused to do what he asked of them, even when he was nice about it. He was a dead weight; the old blood from last night was stuck in his top half and he felt like a worm cut in two.

He tested his legs. They still did as they were told and he braced his bare feet against the sides of the bore. They slipped a few times and he stayed where he was. Then he remembered that inside all guns, big or small, there was *rifling* in the barrel. These grooves in the metal spiralled up, round and round inside the gun, spinning the shell to its target. Phil had explained it to him. He'd shown him his pistol that he'd brought home from his war and Bully had looked down it and seen the little grooves shining in the darkness, and pictured someone dying at the end of it.

Bully didn't want to be dying *inside* a gun, and he lifted his knees up a little, felt for the grooves with his toes and then jammed them in as far as they would go. And he pushed and pushed … and slowly, slowly he shuffled himself and Jack back up the barrel.

A few seconds after he got his elbows hooked over the lip of the gun, the pins and needles started poking into him, and he was a long time writhing about and complaining about it, saying *Jesus wet, Jesus wet*, even though he was drying out now.

He remembered then the man's scream from a few hours ago and he looked down around him. And there he was, that man, lying on the ground. His pockets were turned inside out and his belly was leaking onto the grass and turning it a dead brown colour. But Bully still watched him for a while longer until he was sure he was dead.

03 20 22
DAYS HOURS MINUTES

When the pain had had enough of him, Bully started climbing out of the barrel. It was easier than getting in because he was getting *out*. It didn't matter how scary it was looking that far down, with a dead man on the ground. He shuffled back along the barrel on his hands and knees, Jack still inside his hoodie. He looked for his trainers and socks but they were gone. And though he squinted up into the grey light, he couldn't see his coat in the tree either. Janks must have taken it, searching for his ticket. Then he remembered what else was in one of his pockets. He stood still a moment, taking it in, mourning the loss of his mum's birthday card.

Today was the first day he would not be hearing her voice since the day she died.

He heard a car roaring past on the empty road, saw its lights still on, showing up the early morning. He got himself moving, walked towards the gates, pretending the dead man wasn't there, but then he looked back, couldn't help it, just to make sure he really was never getting up again.

03 **20** **14**
DAYS HOURS MINUTES

On the road he got his bearings from the compass on his penknife. He watched the little arrow point north and made his way towards the river. He didn't have any money or any food or even any shoes. But all he had to do was just keep following the arrow to get to Watford and Camelot, and then he could buy as much food and as many pairs of Reeboks as he liked. The geeky guy had told him Watford was about twenty miles away, north of London. That sounded a lot but then he thought about how much walking he did most days just wandering round. And he was bound to bump into Watford if he just carried on walking north, at least to see a sign for it or find a train going that way.

First of all, though, he had to get across the river.

London was empty. Nothing much was moving. Even the river was sludgy and slow. He walked past the Eye, stared at the grey, empty pods hanging from the whitening sky. It *was* broken now, nothing going round.

"Jack!" he yelled because Jack was off chasing pigeons still sleeping on the ground. And then he looked around as the buildings across the river threw his own voice back at him. All around him it was like TV with the sound right down, making him nervy and twisting him around. Basically, the quiet was too LOUD and he felt like the last boy in the world and he wanted the zombies back, pouring out of the station and across the bridge so that he could lose himself among them.

He wondered then if it would be better to wait longer, to hide out until it got busier or even until Monday morning before he crossed. But the tourists didn't turn up until the middle of the day and Monday was too far away and he felt the urge to make a run for it *now*.

He knew if he didn't get across now, the more chance they had of hunting him down, of picking up his scent again on this side of the river. And even if Janks didn't use his dog, humans could still hunt. All Janks and his crew had to do was look for a boy without shoes and socks and a funny-looking dog. Even in London that wouldn't be hard to find.

* * *

He got to the end of the footpath that ran alongside the river and then on his hands and knees he crawled up the steps to the road bridge above. He heard a car coming and ducked down, waiting long after the tyres had gone, until the smell of the exhaust disappeared. Then he peeped his eyes up just above the top step, so that anyone looking would just see half a head. When he saw the road bridge it looked much longer than he remembered because it was closer and emptier than he'd ever seen it before. There were, he reckoned, two or three football pitches in distance between him and Big Ben. And though he was thirsty and his eyes were heating up whilst the rest of him was getting cold, he waited. And he waited. And he watched the long hand shudder towards the end of the hour, getting ready to bang on to the whole of London that it was four o'clock on a Sunday morning.

He ducked down as another car raced past, making time on the straight through roads. Then, like he was going to hold his breath for a very long time, he took a deep one and decided this was it. He stood up and began to run across the bridge towards Big Ben, the clock face getting bigger as he ran.

He was running jinksy because of his ankle and kept veering off into the road. Once he tripped over Jack and swore at her for getting in his way. Two cars passed them on the bridge. It frightened him, the first one, going ever so, *ever* so slow, like it was going to stop, but it didn't.

Bang... Bang... Bang... Bang... through his head, like Big Ben was punishing him for taking so long to cross the river. And when the banging stopped and he took his hands away from his ears and looked up, a *huge* fat man wrapped in a big black coat with a stick was looking down at him.

CHURCHILL it said underneath the statue.

He was pretty sure he'd heard of him: something to do with winning one of the wars with a big I in it. He looked nice and warm up there, all wrapped up. Bully missed his coat, still felt the loss of it and what was in it.

He stopped all that when he heard the noise of the motorbike revving up along the river. He didn't know why he was frightened of the motorbike, why it was making him want to hide. Perhaps because all he'd heard so far this morning had been cars. Perhaps because it sounded louder than the cars, louder than most bikes, like a trail bike, something *off*-road that didn't really belong in the city, that could go after him on the pavement, through parks and wherever he went.

The bike was going slow but getting closer … the sound of a fat two-stroke engine buffeting the buildings around him, pistons poking up and down…

Rummm … rummm …. rummmm… Rummmmmm…

Bully looked round the square. There were old buildings everywhere but nothing to crawl up, no doorways to hide in, and the politician place was wrapped up in iron railings and locked away, looking like a one-off, very pricey giant sandcastle. He took another look around the square. He'd been so busy scouting the buildings he hadn't really taken in what was there. In the middle on the grass were a crowd of green and brown tents and for just a silly second he thought maybe they were there on holiday. Then he saw the coloured rags and signs tied to the trees at the edge of the pavement.

PEACE CAMP

He knew where he was then: crustie town. He'd heard about the protesters, living on the pavements and getting in everyone's way, moaning on all day and night about soldiers killing people. But right this second he loved crusties! He was glad they were there, camped out in the middle of the Big Ben square! And he ran into the little tent town to hide. And when he realized the sound of the bike was steady and very soon he would see it, and they would see *him*, he whispered: "Down, girl! Down!" And he followed Jack to the ground.

On his knees and elbows he worked his way towards one of the tents at the edge of the camp. He snatched a look between the little *V* shaped gaps in the tents and it *was* a dirt bike, big, curling mudguards and rocked-up suspension. And he could see two men: one driving, one riding pillion with his visor up, looking around, *really* searching, his crash helmet going left and right … left and right. Neither one was Janks's shape and size.

The bike slowly circled the camp and Bully slowly crawled round the tent, Jack staying with him, keeping on the bike's blind side. He patted the fabric to see if anyone was in there. No one said anything and when he got to the front he unzipped it and dived in, ready to plead for just a minute, for just enough time to get his breath back… But the tent was empty.

"In, in," he said to Jack before the bike went past, but as he pulled the zip back up he heard the engine idle and then stop.

He waited. The men were talking quietly but not whispering. He took a breath, let it out slowly, put a little early morning mist inside the tent.

"What did you see?"

"I dunno. Something moving. Something over there. I can't see shit through this visor. D'you wanna swap?"

"Which tent was it?"

"I *dunno*. I just said, *over there*. They all look the same. Over that way."

"This is a waste of time! What is it exactly that he's got, anyway? What did Janks say?"

"He wouldn't say, would he? Must be sumin' that's worth a bit."

"Maybe we get it out of the boy and it's worth a *lot*."

"Suits me, but we gotta find 'im first…"

So there was a price stickered up on his head now,

thought Bully. And Janks had put it there. How many people knew about his lottery ticket? How many mobiles were ringing now, tagged with his name? He didn't want to think about it – frightened him too much.

He could hear them walking about, one of them tripping and swearing. "Shh," he said, because Jack was panting quicker and louder than he was. Then he heard a tent zip go zithering down near by. Then another.

"This one's empty... And this one... There's no one 'ere, Baz!"

That set him shivering all over again. Crustie town was just like any other town: they went home for the weekend. He heard another zip go, closer in. Another and another. And then *bumpth ... bumpth...* They were booting the tents over now. It was quicker and more of a laugh.

Bumpth ... bumpth...

"Arrgh!"

Someone was inside the tent next door to his!

"What do you think you're *doing*!"

A woman was going for them, yelling, calling them *fascists*. And they were yelling back, telling her to *go back to sleep, love*. But now more hippies were waking up and joining in. The place wasn't empty after all, just *half* empty. And the two men were effing and blinding, backing away to their bike.

He heard the engine rev up and go. And when he stopped hearing the bike, he wobbled over to the zip on his knees, pulled it down slowly and peeked out. The hippies were all looking in one direction still, the way the bike had gone, north out of the square. One or two were rubbing their heads, and saying it was *unbelievable*. After a while they started picking up tents and putting them back like it had just been a stupid game.

Bully zipped his tent back up and he relaxed then and had a look round inside it.

He had never been in a tent before and didn't think much of it: the walls were only thin and moved when you touched them and he didn't think it was much better than sleeping out.

There was a sleeping bag but no water, just a rolled-up banner and some rubbish in a plastic bag. He had a look through it anyway. He could do with something to drink but what he *really* needed right now was a wee. So he waited for all the crusties and hippies to go back to bed and then pulled the zip down just a little…

And for the first time in a long while, he giggled.

03 **12** **34**
DAYS HOURS MINUTES

Peace not war! Peace not war! Peace not war! Peace not war! Peace not war! Peace not war!

The shouting and whistling woke him up in a panic. He wondered where he was, the soft green ceiling of the tent warming his face just a few centimetres away. He'd been out for the count. He'd expected Big Ben to wake him up like an alarm clock when it got to five or six in the morning but he'd slept through all that *bang, banging* of the clock... He stopped thinking about it when he caught a sort of thick burnt-chocolatey stench working through his cold—

"Jack! Jesus *wet*."

Jack did her sorry face, looking sideways at the ground. She'd had to go and she'd done it as far away from Bully as she could ... but in a two-man tent that wasn't very far away.

Bully tried to breathe just through his mouth but a backlog of phlegm made him gag. He listened to the hullabaloo outside. He couldn't go out there in all that noise just yet, he didn't know what was going down. So he emptied out the rubbish bag from the corner, and for the first time in his life he picked *it* up.

He put a knot in the bag and flung it away. Then he checked Jack's collar. The chewing-gum hadn't set yet and he rubbed a little bit more grease and dirt into it. Then he sat still to work things out. He estimated by the feel of the light and the way the sun was hitting the tent it was well past getting-up and making-a-move time. Maybe 11.00 or 12.00. He couldn't hear any cars, just voices, a *lot* of them, shouting and moving about like a big, big party going on out there. Sometimes they'd had them on his estate, out on the grass between the blocks, in the summer, with burgers and drinks and laughing and... A drum started up and then more shouting and he put his hands to his ears for a bit.

Peace not war! Peace not war! Peace not war!

When the drum stopped, he had a look out, unzipping the tent enough for one eye to get the light. *All* the crusties and hippies had come back. And they'd brought their friends, too. The square had been transformed from a campsite into a full-on holiday camp ... hundreds, maybe thousands of people shouting and singing and looking *really* happy about it, even with their faces screwed up and angry. They weren't a problem but the Feds were... They were *all* round the square, blocking off *all* the exits.

He swore a lot, had a think while he was doing it and then got his penknife out and had a look at the compass. He shuffled round on his knees until he was facing roughly north, then he slit the side of the tent with the short blade of his knife. He was on the edge of the camp and he could see the Feds had set up special barriers at the exits, standing right next to each other so no one could get through, flashes of sunlight coming off their high-vis jackets. He thought it was sunlight until the light showed up too white and sharp and *snappy* and he looked again: the Feds were taking photos of everyone leaving the square. He didn't want anyone knowing he was here. He didn't want no publicity.

How was he going to get out? He didn't want to wait here all day until they took the barriers away. It wasn't just the time he was wasting; he didn't like the feeling of being stuck somewhere, as if he was in an open prison. He had to get going. Bully knew if he wanted to get out of the square without any trouble, he would have to blend in. And to blend in, he needed *camouflage*. He needed to look like everyone else. Problem was, he didn't. He put his head back in the tent and looked at as much of himself as he could from the neck down.

For a start he was dirty, filthy all over, and he had no socks, no shoes, just a scabby hoodie and jeans that weren't cool and ripped, just *worn out*. He looked exactly like what he was: living on the pavement. And his long straggly hair had nothing in it to make it smooth and new-looking. He knew he just didn't look right. He had to change.

He took his hoodie off because Feds didn't like hoodies and there was no point hiding underneath one because they would stop him straight away and want to see his face. Then he started work on his jeans. He took them off too, cut each leg away above the knee and burned the ends with his lighter to give them a crustie look. He put them back on. He'd cut off too much and they were a bit too *high* and getting near his bum but at least he didn't look *so* homeless now. None of his mates wore shorts, not on the streets, not even when it was hot. Not even the Daveys, cracked in the head, wore shorts. Next he gave himself a bit of a wash, hawked up what was left of the green stuff until he had a clean mouthful of bubbly – spit was like soapy water if you thought about it – and he rubbed off the worst bits of dirt that he could see. Finally, he combed through his hair with his nails and then smoothed it back with his wet hands.

Still, though, he didn't think it would be good enough. His cut-offs showed up his skinny white legs and made him look younger. And he didn't have shoes. He had to be honest with himself: without his coat and hat, he didn't look old enough to be even a shrunk-up, grown-up crustie boy. And he was forgetting something… What was he going to do about Jack? As soon as the Feds saw her they would start asking *What sort of dog is that? Are you the owner?* Everyone asked him that. And you had to be sixteen to own a dog. It said so in his magazines. And then they would start taking a second look at *him*, asking the same sort of questions. What sort of person was he? Was he *really* sixteen? Did his parents know he was here? Where was he from? Who owned him? And then he'd never get to Camelot, never see his money.

He put the problem of his age to one side and for a few minutes he tried to think of ways of hiding Jack. There was nothing to put her in. So he had a go at wrapping her up in his hoodie but her long grey-and-white snout kept poking out and anyway, the Feds might think she was some sort of terror threat, a *dog bomb*. So he took his hoodie and tied it round his waist. Then he untied it and put it round his shoulders to make him look wider like the bouncers in the tunnel but it just made him look like a *girl*. What else could he do? There was nothing else in the tent, just this *crustie stuff*. He had nothing on him except his lighter, Jack's dog lead and half a dozen rubber bands on his wrists.

He had another look and *still* there was nothing in the tent but rubbish and dog shit and the banner. He unrolled the banner. Someone might be coming for it soon to hold it up, he thought. It didn't have any writing on it, just a picture of a big red missile blowing up a little white pigeon with a twig in its beak.

"Errgh," he said because the paint was oily and wet and coming off on his fingers.

And then he had a weird, brilliant idea to get out of the square, so brilliant that it was as if someone else had thought of it and told him about it. And so weird he could only imagine someone else pulling it off.

It wasn't *camouflage* exactly…

But how was he going to get Jack out? Then he had a thought: maybe he wasn't going to get Jack out. He looked into her eyes. Sometimes he felt like she was older than him not just in dog years but in human ones too, like she knew more about him than he did.

He lay on his belly and looked out the back of the tent again to scope out the sightline and see what he could see.

"Come 'ere, mate," he said. And he got a hold of her head and worked his fingers around her tight collar. He took it off. He felt bad about this.

"All righ' then… All right, mate… Listen, mate…" He put on his kindest voice, the one he saved just for dogs nowadays. And Jack made a noise like she was trying to eat invisible meat, as if she was chewing over what he was saying.

"OK. Look … mate. Look. Now stay … stay…" he said as gently and calmly as he could, though the final words still came out as a squeak. "You got to *stay*…"

10

03 DAYS **11** HOURS **43** MINUTES

The two policemen in charge of the north exit had been there since the barriers had come off the back of the lorry first thing that morning. And now it was getting on for midday and the sun was burning through the cloud, they were getting hot underneath their stab-proof vests.

"You're going to be there for a while," the officer warned the couple at the head of the queue, waiting to get into the demonstration. It was one in one out like in a nightclub at capacity and the police officers were stopping the new protesters coming in and checking their bags for bombs and sharp instruments and other *illicit* material.

"You don't mind, do you, Luke, if we go in separately?" the girl said to her boyfriend. "It's only just started and you won't have to wait long."

He shrugged like he did a bit, because he'd only just started going out with her, but he didn't want to say anything in front of the policemen.

"Why do we have to be caged up like this anyway? It's like a protest *zoo* you've put us in," he said to the officer so he didn't have to answer his girlfriend's question.

"Section 60. Criminal Justice and Public Order Act. Your health, our safety," he said in a sing-song way because he'd been making the same joke all morning.

Luke looked round, conscious now of the queue of people building up behind him, waiting to get in to protest against the war on the other side of the world. On the other side of the barrier there was a much shorter line of people trying to get out. One teenage girl at the front, looking embarrassed, like she was thinking of changing her mind and staying put. Luke didn't think she looked quite right for a protest in bare feet with her cut-offs and *Transformers* T-shirt; more a festival vibe, he thought – especially with that belt clipped round her waist. And he gave her a disapproving look because peace was a serious business.

"Look, let's just leave it for now, Becky, OK. I don't want to lose you or anything. Why don't we come back later? We can see it from over there anyway." Luke pointed back towards St James's Park and they stood out of the way to let the man behind through. But even though this man didn't have any bags to search, the officer still stopped him.

"Just a minute, sir. Can we let this young lady out first, please…" He nodded to the girl, her shoulder-length, wet-look hair tied back with a couple of elastic bands, the sort that postal workers regularly discarded on their rounds.

"Oh, mind your toes, miss," he said when he saw her bare feet. "There's broken glass all over the place." And then he smiled because he had a daughter himself, a few years younger than this girl, who looked about sixteen or seventeen though he couldn't be sure, the way girls made themselves up nowadays. He hoped his own daughter would use a little less lipstick when she got to this age.

He waved the girl through and she was about to move off when the second officer put up his hand.

"Just a minute, love. Do you mind if we take your photo?"

The girl went very shy then.

"You don't have to let them, you know," said Becky, still there. "You can say no, it's not against the law to say no."

But the girl just nodded meekly while a third policeman took her picture. "Can you lift your head up … a bit more … a bit more… Lovely… What's your name?"

"Jacky… Jacky Bradley."

"Nice name," he said, as he said to all the girls, and he let her go. And the next man went through into the square.

A few seconds later, safely on the other side of the police line, the same girl jumped up on a bench and shouted in a rough squeak: "Here, mate! Here, Jack!" She put a finger from each hand to her mouth and tried to whistle.

"Jack! Here! Here! Come on!"

"Someone's lost their boyfriend!" a voice piped up and a few people laughed along at the edge of the good-natured crowd.

"Here, Jacky! Here, girl!" yelled the girl, her voice breaking up, stopping short.

"Oi! Come on … let's have you down from there," said the first officer, seeing her up on the bench, and she screwed up her face, looking much less pretty now, and stayed where she was, stretching up on one foot. He was about to go and have serious words about health and safety when he heard rising laughter and a few shrieks coming from inside the peace camp. He turned back and saw fingers pointing and the crowd parting. People were looking down at their feet and jumping sideways like an earthquake was putting a crack in the road. And then he saw a funny-looking dog with a face full of teeth galloping out of the square straight for the north exit barrier.

The police officer got out his baton in case it went for his ankles but on its last stride it sat back on its hind legs and sprang – more like a cat than a dog – giving everything it had to clear four feet of galvanized steel, *just* skimming the top of the barrier, its front legs going ten to the dozen like it was doing doggy-paddle in mid-air. He got ready to give it a wallop but the dog wasn't going for him. It went through the crowd queuing to get in and skidded to a halt underneath the girl on the bench. And the girl gave him a final twist of her face and then jumped down and ran off, one leg a little wonky, the dog following along after her.

"Funny-looking pair," he said, watching them head north towards the lake in St James's Park. And he put away his baton.

03 **11** **06**
DAYS HOURS MINUTES

Bully tried to wipe the oily red paint off his lips with the back of his hand but he just smeared it more and more because he didn't have any spit left, so in the end he got Jack to lick his face and wiped it on his hoodie.

"Good girl, good girl!" He kept telling her that, over and over again. He had never read anything like it in all his magazines (and that included *Modern Dogs* and *Dogs World* and *Dogs Now*). Not in any of them had he heard of a dog staying like that. At that distance. With all that noise. Running through all those crusties and hippies in the square. And getting through a line of Feds too! He should get her a treat. He had an old bit of chewing-gum in his pocket but that was worse than chocolate for dogs so he put it in his own mouth instead.

He got his compass out again, careful to hide the knife, some Feds still hanging about on the road. Straight north to Camelot from here wasn't possible; there was a long lake in the middle of the park and he would have to go round it first. So he shadowed the wide straight road lined with trees, keeping a lookout for motorbikes and for cars that were moving slow, not trying to get somewhere fast like the rest of London was.

And besides, it was easier on his feet on the grass. As a rule, back at his place, he never took his shoes off, even at night. And he thought about his place then and missed it – half wished he was back there, going through his usual routine without his millions to think about, just maybe something extra to eat. Because his life was more messed up now than it had been before. He had never thought money could do that. Make things more complicated, maybe even worse. It seemed to make things easier and better for footballers and celebrities. And even if they got chased it was only for a photo. It wasn't serious. And it wasn't with dogs. And no one got stabbed to death in a park.

Perhaps when he had the money in his hands, throwing it up in the air like millionaires did at least once a day, perhaps when he had a chance to *spend* it, then every single thing in his life might start to get simpler and better.

He took his hoodie off his shoulders and put it back on. He never went anywhere in just a T-shirt. He didn't feel safe or right, like he was missing the top layer of his skin. He went to pull the elastic bands off his hair but then he changed his mind. It occurred to him that anyone looking for him and looking *at* him might still think he was a girl. And though this was bad because he was a boy, it was worth putting up with for a while longer if it put them off the scent. He comforted himself that it was practical: that it kept the hair out of his eyes and ears and in kung fu films the men wore it clubbed like that too.

He heard Jack doing her thirsty panting. He saw her licking at the wet grass in the shadows and then eating it, too. Guilt put a stop to Bully's escape celebrations. He thought about what Jack had been through, all that waiting she'd done in the hot green tent, not knowing if Bully was coming back. And dogs got stressed, that was a fact. It upset him now to think of it – how he'd done that to his dog – and he started scouting out for water, trying to make it up to her.

There was water in the lake but he only ever fed Jack clean

water, the same as humans. Generally speaking (except for dog food) if it wasn't good enough for him, it wasn't good enough for Jack. He spied a drinking fountain further along the path, tourists queuing with their rucksacks strapped to their fronts like they were going to blow themselves up. He pulled a crackled plastic bottle out of a bin and queued up, got to the front quick with Jack there, a couple of the girls looking frightened because she was sniffing their ankles, logging their smell as friendly among the billions and trillions of London smells. He filled his bottle up and then he put his thumb over the spout of the fountain.

"Water. Here, mate, open up," he said. Jack opened her mouth and Bully squirted the water and the girls surprised him then by clapping like it was a trick. He thought about asking for money like the street performers did, but when he held out his hand the girls walked away and all he got was a lick from Jack on his shins. He bent down and patted her, scratched the little brown ring of fur between her ears and around her neck that stopped her being streaky white and grey all over.

He panicked for a second when he didn't see her collar but then remembered he'd taken it off just in case and put it in his back pocket. He checked his pockets. But there was nothing there. He checked the others. Nothing. A chainsaw of horror started up in Bully's head as he clumsily went from one pocket to the next, refusing to believe it was gone. It was God punishing him and Jesus too for even thinking that Jack might not make it out of the square. He should never have left her. He should never have taken her collar off. He promised he would never do that again, but the collar still wasn't in his back pocket.

He turned round and screwed up his eyes and stared back along the path through the tourists, but there was no strip of leather lying on the ground. He started running back, dodging round people at the last minute because he had his head down, yelling at them to get out the way. One man didn't. He came wobbling straight at him and they both dodged the same way.

"What the…?" yelled Bully, scrambling up onto his feet.

"Sorry, sorry…" said the man, holding his hand up like he needed help and waving and shouting at Bully to come back. He could wave all he wanted, thought Bully, and then he heard a familiar *jingle-jangle*.

"I saw you… I saw the dog…"

Bully ignored him and snatched the collar out of his hand. He examined it *just* in case the guy was trying to rip him off.

"We were just getting ice creams and I saw it on the ground and then I looked back – and my wife said she'd seen…" He paused to substitute a more suitable word than his wife had used to sum Bully up. "*Someone*. Someone with a dog—"

He stopped his explanation then, to wipe his forehead. Bully could see way back down the path a blurry line-up of three or four suspects that might be a family waiting for this man to rejoin them.

"I'll give you a million quid," he suddenly said to the man. He wanted him to have it.

"Ha ha. Well, thanks. I could do with that," said the man awkwardly.

"I will! I'll give it to yer! When I get *my* money! I'll give you a million quid, mate!"

"Ha ha," he laughed nervously. And the man noticed Bully didn't have any shoes and thought perhaps his wife's description of the boy had been pretty accurate after all. "It's really OK. I'm just glad you got it back."

"You can have it! In a couple of days! I'm on my way!"

"Thank you. It's fine. Really. Whatever it is, you keep it."

Bully watched him turn back into a zombie. He could see in his face that getting-away look that zombies gave you, regretting the good thing they'd done if you started trying to talk to them too much like they were human beings.

"Don't worry. I'm just glad I could help," he said.

"Your loss, mate," said Bully, watching him trot back to his family like he didn't want to be seen running. And Bully shrugged to show everyone that it *was* the man's loss. And having just saved himself a million quid, he knelt down and carefully put Jack's collar back on.

"Sorry, mate," he said. "I won't take it off again."

He carried on further along the grass, drinking and thinking and keeping an eye on his compass, following it west but getting ready to go north the moment the lake ran out of water and he could get across to the other side of the park. He couldn't hear the noise from the demonstration any more and he saw between the trees a white stone bridge and then, right in the middle of nowhere, the queen's house.

He'd been meaning to come and have a look one day and now it was *this* day.

He had to give it to her: it looked *big*, way bigger than on TV. He tried counting all the windows but lost interest when he got past twenty. He liked the flag on the roof best but there was no helicopter up there or swimming pool that he could see. His place would be better than this. He'd have slides coming out of his windows down to the ground – not water slides just slidy slides – so he wouldn't have to take the stairs or the lift. It got on his nerves in every block he'd ever lived in, always taking so long to get *out*.

He went closer, stepping out of the park and onto the pavement towards the great big wedding cake roundabout outside the palace gates. He tried to mix in with the day-tripping zombies but wherever Jack went she created a little circle of fear, marking them out from the crowd. He stood there for a good five minutes, curious to see the queen. A lot of the zombies were doing the same thing, just staring and taking pictures of what they couldn't see.

His mum loved the queen. All the diamonds and fur coats she had, all those spare bedrooms that didn't get taxed. Phil wasn't so keen: the princes were all *flyboys*, not one of them had taken a bullet for his country *on the ground*.

He gave the queen a few more minutes but she didn't turn up. Probably her day off, he thought, being a Sunday. And with his last look at the palace his gaze dropped down to a silver car going round the roundabout. He noted the plates, the last three letters – **REX** – looking like a dog's name from olden times. The window was down. In the driver's seat was a guy in sunglasses and a brown shirt, his arm out, resting on the door, a ciggy cupped in the palm of his hand so that it didn't blow out.

A big old-fashioned double-decker bus with the top ripped off was coming up to the roundabout. It stopped at the zebra crossing for the zombies. And Bully watched the car go round the roundabout for a second time, the ciggy still cupped in the man's hand … too busy looking around to take another pull on it…

Probably nothing. Still: *Better safe than dead*, Phil always said.

Bully waited until the open-top bus began to pull away and then ran along beside it. And then, when he saw there was no conductor downstairs, he picked up Jack, sped up as best he could with his ankle, and holding his dog under one arm, he made a grab for the pole.

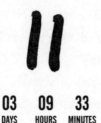

03 **09** **33**
DAYS HOURS MINUTES

The car turned off the roundabout away from the palace and was heading along the Mall when the Snapback spotted the boy, saw him jumping on the bus with a whole dog under his arm.

"That's him! There, there! There! On the bus. Quick, quick, he's going to Piccadilly! Don't lose him! Do a U-ey!"

"All right, Snapback. I heard you first time." Terry flicked his fag onto the road, did a U-turn.

"Punch it then! Punch it!" said the Snapback. And Terry stepped on the *loud* pedal ... lurched forward and stalled. A policeman began walking over to have words just as he got the car going again and pulled away.

"He didn't get the number, did he?" whined the Snapback.

Terry shrugged. He didn't care. It was the Snapback's car. He'd teamed up with this guy for the job because he *had* a car. A friend of a friend of Janks. He didn't like his stupid name, so he called him *Snapback* because his stupid baseball cap said *Man U*. And Terry didn't like his football team, either. He'd already told him this a good few times today. Terry could do

127

that because he was the muscle. He could say whatever he liked.

"You sure it was 'im?"

"Yeah, yeah. It was definitely him. He was carrying a dog. I saw it under his arm!"

"Under his arm? You sure?"

"Yeah!" And he got out his phone and showed him the picture that had come with the reward message as if that proved something.

"You'd better be right. Make me *happy*," said Terry.

Last night he *had* been happy with a few drinks in him, thinking about this big reward money, but now the drink was draining out of him it was beginning to feel like a long shot. And that was making him *un*happy. And when he felt like that he liked to threaten people so that they weren't happy either. Why did Janks want the boy, though? He wasn't saying, but Terry had an idea. He'd heard a few whispers on the grapevine about a *prize* ticket. Now if this was *the* boy with *that* ticket, then it was a long shot worth risking anyone's happiness for.

He put his foot down, accelerated until he was almost touching the bumper of the car in front. The bus was three cars away, so Terry overtook them in one go, making the oncoming traffic brake. The car behind him beeped and Terry leaned out the window, swivelled his head and stared at a spot on the windscreen where the driver's head would normally be, until the car stopped beeping and slowed right down.

"OK, Snapback, you listening?" said Terry. "At the next

traffic lights, you jump out and get on the bus and get him *off*. And I'll pull over and grab him and stick him in the boot. Right?"

"Won't someone see us?"

"Yeah, but so what? He's a nobody."

The Snapback twitched a little while he thought about all this jumping out of cars and onto buses. And then he said, "Why don't I take over driving and you get on the bus?"

Terry took off his sunglasses. He leaned over and gave him the same look he'd given the car behind, but without sunglasses blanking out his eyes it was much meaner and nastier and *closer*.

03 09 31
DAYS HOURS MINUTES

"On your left you can see Buckingham Palace Gardens where the queen hosts her many garden parties during the summer months..."

Upstairs the conductor was giving a guided tour to the zombies. It sounded packed up there, feet clomping about, everyone wanting to see out on a nice day. Bully was sat at the back, out of sight of the bus driver's rear-view mirror. No one had noticed him jumping on. The seats at the back were empty and there were just seven or eight wig heads sat at the front, not able to get up the stairs.

He settled down. According to his compass the bus was going north and that worked for him, for a while.

When he heard the beeping he looked round and saw the silver car up the bus's backside. He couldn't see the driver until the big man in the brown shirt poked his head out. And then he didn't want to see him because his eyes were popped white full of dollar signs.

"*On your right is Green Park … once common ground and a swampy burial ground used for lepers. It was enclosed in the seventeenth century and bought by Charles II…*"

He willed the bus to go faster but whenever he looked out the back by the stairs, the car was still there.

The bus slowed… A skinny guy in a red snapback jumped out of the silver car and ran for the bus, his legs going faster than the rest of him. Bully got ready to kick at his fingers if he made a grab for the pole. He could see the snapback working out the distance he had to jump … but the bus sped up and the snapback slowed down and banged on the side of the car to get back in.

They were going to rush him, grab him at the next set of lights – that's what they had planned, he thought. And without thinking too much about what he was going to do, Bully grabbed a pushchair from among the luggage tucked under the steps that wound up to the top floor. And then he threw it off the bus.

It bounced once on the tarmac, opened up and the air got into it and it flew over the roof of the car. The car swerved but didn't slow down. Bully pulled out a big grey suitcase half his size and trundled it to the edge of the step … and pushed it off. It ricocheted off the kerb and under one of the wheels, making the car jump but it carried on driving.

He needed to aim better. The big suitcase had been too heavy to throw at the right angle, so he grabbed a couple of smaller pieces of luggage and threw them, one after the other, with a straight arm like he was lobbing grenades. The first missed but the second one *exploded* onto the windscreen. He thought that might do it. The glass cracked up and pushed in but the wipers started going and the snapback was leaning out the window, like an extra windscreen wiper, pulling off clothes, shouting to the driver…

"Stop it! You naughty boy!" The wig heads at the front of the bus were looking at him, one of them standing, shouting at him. He ignored them all and yanked out a big green rucksack like the one Phil had in the army. But he held on to it, didn't throw it. He looked back under the stairs. He was down to light ammunition – a couple of umbrellas, a coat – but then he saw collapsed up against the side one last thing…

The bus driver braked hard when he saw the wheelchair bouncing off the back of his bus. And when he did, he felt a thud as the car behind went straight into the back of him.

Bang!

Bully saw it coming, was holding on to the pole, but Jack wasn't and she skidded down between the seats. The silver car started whining away in reverse and Bully grabbed the rucksack.

"Was that you?" said the conductor on the stairs. He was just standing there as if waiting for Bully to say *Yeah!* and own up to it. Instead he jumped off the bus, dragging the rucksack with him.

In mid-air he shouted, "Here girl!" and the conductor stood well back as a gnashy-looking dog scuttled past and followed her master off the back of the bus.

03 **09** **24**
DAYS HOURS MINUTES

The bus conductor tried chasing Bully to Piccadilly but he was fat and slow and Bully easily got away, even with the weight of the rucksack on his back.

Now in a side street, he was taking a look. He started pulling out clothes. It was women's stuff – dresses and tops and other things that were no good to him. Because all he was looking for were shoes. He needed shoes if he was going to walk to Watford. Even if he managed to get the train, he still needed to look *half* decent to convince a nice lady or someone old enough to cash his ticket in for him. Because no one *nice* was going to believe a word he said unless he had shoes on his feet.

Halfway through the rucksack he found something, although it wasn't exactly what he'd had in mind: flip-flops. He was pretty sure they were girls' too, purple and yellow with a swirly flowery design on them, but they would have to do. He shoved his toes in them and finished emptying out the rest of the clothes. Right at the bottom he found money. It wasn't *real* money though; it had a drawing of a skinny guy with Harry Potter glasses on the front. *Bank of India* it said. No good to him and he threw it all away.

When he'd emptied out the rucksack, he put it on the ground and told Jack to get in.

Jack looked at him like: *What, you mean in* there? But this was the other reason he'd nicked it – to hide Jack, so that he wasn't a boy with a dog, he was a boy with a rucksack. Bully got her rear end and pushed her in and then got her settled and pulled the top flap down, leaving a gap for her to breathe through. He could still just about see her snout and eyes like this rucksack had a … well, a dog in it.

He put it on. He adjusted the straps. It wasn't too bad. And he set off north to Camelot thinking about his money just waiting to be spent, begging and pleading with him to go to the shops and spend, spend, spend…

Flip, flop… *Flip*, flop, *flip*, flop. He kept looking back every few steps for the men in the silver car. He wasn't used to the sound of his own feet under him, and he turned round to check it was *him* flip-flopping along.

He got to Oxford Street. Not the back of it but right on it, his first time there. And he thought of poor old Mick squashed up pulpy in the back of the bin truck. The last bin he was ever going to kip in.

Bully walked along. It was one long street full of shops. He shielded his eyes from the sun. He imagined Brent Cross was like this but better, with a roof on. That was the place to go said Chris and Tiggs. Everything you needed under one roof.

He stopped the first woman who looked like she could

be a mum – softer-looking than the younger women carrying big-name bags with next to nothing in them. And she was carrying food not clothes in plastic bags like mums did.

"Have you got 59—" he asked but she was already walking away. He carried on along the street and after asking directions and begging for a while he'd managed to get three quid off foreigners. But no one knew anything, where anywhere was. No one lived here, on Oxford Street, in London. He thought maybe he should get a map, rack one up from a bookshop, just to check what that guy had said about Watford was right.

He carried on walking through alleyways and along little roads until he got to a big nasty one, four lanes thick, sunshine *blowtorching* the windows and windscreens. *Mary le Bone* it said on the side of one of the buildings. He could see the gates of another park through the gaps in the buildings and he walked along, getting ready to cross this tarmac river, thinking about buying a helicopter – no, better than that – a jetpack. He'd seen them on TV – not just in films, either, but in real-life programmes. And the pack wasn't much bigger than the rucksack he had on now. He could light it up, stick Jack on the back and *go*.

He imagined flying just above the pavements, not too high so everyone else walking along could look up and see him and think: *I wish I had one of those…* And deciding what he'd buy with his money reminded him of the foreign money he'd thrown away. It hit him that even on Sunday he could have changed it for *proper* money at a bank or some place… And then bought a map and food and a cold can of Coke…

In the middle of telling himself off and reminding himself again of just what else he had lost today, he stepped off the pavement and something picked him up, shook him hard and threw him down the road.

13

03 DAYS   **07** HOURS   **54** MINUTES

He was paralyzed. He couldn't breathe. He lay on his side, his eyes stuck staring at the creases and wrinkles in the tarmac, willing the air back into his lungs. He'd felt like this once before, lying in a bundle, buried above ground, three or four older boys jumping him in the changing rooms. He'd never liked PE, running round for the sake of it, getting tired out for nothing, playing games where you didn't win anything worth keeping. At least when you played the arcades, whatever you won or lost was yours. And it was real, it was something…

And then he felt his breath slowly coming back, like he was having to suck it out of someone else's body.

"Arrgh…" he said, the hurt catching up with him. He got into a crouch and then sat up, hugging his knees. A rusted white van was moving away, reversing, now pulling round him and going through the gears. Another car began driving towards him and then pulled up. Horns started beeping but the man got out.

"Are you all right?" the man said, wondering what to do if the boy said no.

Bully nodded, didn't waste his new breath saying yes.

"You sure? He just *hit you* – stay there and I'll phone an ambulance. OK?"

Bully told himself to get up. "Get up," he said. And he did – onto his hands and knees and then up onto two legs. He felt light-headed and then just *light*. And though he still had the rucksack on, something wasn't right.

"Is that anything to do with you?" said the guy, pointing uncertainly behind Bully.

He turned round to face the sun and Jack was lying on the road behind him, twitching.

"You did that! You did it!"

"I didn't… I just stopped. I… I… I didn't even see it." And he went pale, hesitated and then got back in his car and drove off slowly with his accident lights still blinking orange and red.

Bully picked Jack up and carried her right across all four lanes, the traffic snarled up, people slowing down, looking to see. By the time he was over, all the necks had twisted enough to see it was just a dog that wasn't moving, and the traffic sped up again.

He laid her down on the empty pavement. "Come on, wake up!" He poured water over her head and tried to squirt some in her mouth but it just seeped out again, darkening the paving-stones.

"I'll get your tea on, Jack… Come on … come on… I'll get you a tin," he said, though he had no tea, nothing on him, not even an empty can now.

"Get up. Come on, get up! Come on, mate… Come on! Get up, girl! Get up … get up, girl…" His voice was breaking, going up and down, sounding young and old within the same word.

Inside his head he was shouting too, at himself for not looking, for not seeing the van. The rucksack had messed up his sight lines and the sun had got in his eyes but that was *no excuse*. He hadn't seen it coming because he'd been too busy thinking about his *money*. Still, though, he had blame to spare for the van driver, racing between the traffic lights. He wanted to chase after the man in the van and smash him up, and he threw the empty water bottle out into the road.

A car beeped at him, a disgusted face passed him by.

Then underneath the groan and roar of the traffic he heard a living sound. And still on his knees, he almost fainted, his body numb like in the gun, but full of pins and needles he was happy to bear, that he didn't want to go away. And he watched Jack get up onto her front legs and then drag the back ones up after her. She shook and wretched and coughed like she'd eaten too much too quick and was going to sick it up, but she stayed on her feet.

"Are you all right? Is that your dog?" Someone there now. A guy in his twenties with the sort of thin, dirty moustache Bully thought he might be getting any day now was looking at him. And a woman kneeling down with blonde hair so clean, he could see the sun through it.

"Yeah, yeah…" he said.

"Have you lost one of your flip-flops? I think I can see it!"

said the man as if it was fish in the water, excited and pleased to have seen such a thing. He waited until the lights changed to retrieve it.

"I don't think you *are* all right," said the woman. "You should *both* get checked out," she said, because Bully was pushing Jack back into the rucksack and dragging it onto his back. It felt twisted up on one side, and he realized it had a metal frame that had taken most of the bash and that was the reason they were both alive.

"Do you want some water?" She was holding out a bottle. He swallowed all of it and then held it up to his face.

"Can I 'ave it?" he asked because his water bottle had been swept down the road.

"Yes, of course. Yes, have it," she said. "Are you sure you're both all right? I think you should go to A and E. You really should, shouldn't he, James?" James just nodded. Bully ignored them and tried to move the rucksack about on his back. It hurt and stung in the middle and he jiggled the weight around on his shoulders from one side to the other like it was too hot.

"I got to get going."

"Where? Do you want us to come with you or anything?"

He looked at them. He was tempted to ask for help, proper help with his ticket and the money. But there were two of them and he didn't have the head to start thinking about splitting it and what was fair to give them. And besides, they maybe looked *too* nice – because whoever helped him would have to pretend it was their ticket. And he didn't think either of them were the type to tell lies. This was his problem: to find someone in the next three days who was *nice enough* to help him do something that wasn't *all* right.

The man was handing him something in a cup. "Do you want a coffee?"

Bully shook his head. He was sick of coffee and being asked if his dog was his.

"D'you need *anything*?" James asked awkwardly.

"You got 59 p?" he said out of habit and the man looked relieved and pleased that he could give him something. And he checked his change and then gave him a fiver.

"Cheers," Bully said. He shoved it in his back pocket. Then he jiggled the rucksack because it was now rubbing on his hip where the frame was twisted.

"Is there anything else we can do for you?" asked the woman, still wanting to help.

"No," he said, looking back across the road. "I got to go."

14

03 **07** **48**
DAYS HOURS MINUTES

Terry bumped the steaming car right up onto the pavement. The Snapback had pulled the wheelchair out of the front grill but the radiator was losing water and overheating. Pedestrians looked … and then looked away.

"Where is he then?" said Terry. He was sweating from the car chase and bits of him he never got to see were getting very *hot* because there was no air conditioning in the car.

"He was *there*," said the Snapback. "I saw him. He must have gone…"

"You *saw* him? That's no good, is it? Where is he *now*?" And to emphasize the difference between the past and the present, Terry knocked the Snapback's cap off so that he didn't have it on *now*. It made him feel happier and cooled him down, too.

"What you doing! Cut it out! I saw him in the first place, didn't I? I'm the only one seeing things!"

"Yeah…" sniffed Terry. He let it hang there, his contempt for whatever the Snapback was seeing. He got out of the car, sat on the bonnet and then clambered up onto the roof and put a Terry-sized dent in it.

"Hey! What you doin'! It's me mum's car!" said the Snapback as if that might make a difference.

"There's something been going on over there," said Terry, sinking further down into the metal roof so that it looked from above as if a giant fist had punched the car. Across the highway he could see a dark patch on the pavement. Maybe blood or something. "What you waiting for then?" he shouted.

The Snapback stayed put and started fidgeting with his mobile. "I want the money for the windscreen and the repairs," he said.

"You'll have to want then, won't ya? Now go take a *look*."

03 07 34
DAYS HOURS MINUTES

He was sure it was the same silver car on the other side of the *Mary le Bone* road. Bully couldn't see how they were tracking him now Jack was out of sight. These men, these friends of Janks's, didn't have dogs and Bully was well out of his territory.

The iron gates to the park were wide open for cars and zombies, and unconsciously he veered away from them, off the road. The sun, with nothing in the way, was heating him up, getting *under* his skin, making him sweat even in the late afternoon. He made his way to the line of trees running alongside the footpath where it was cooler, a light wind blowing against the back of his head. He tried to keep the weight off his right side where the car had pushed his ribs in. But every time he turned round to check whether anyone was on his tail, it rubbed a little more of the skin off his hips.

A trickle of something wet ran down his neck, and walking along, he couldn't decide if it was sweat or blood.

"You OK, mate? You all right in there, mate?" He could hear Jack panting, trying to cool herself down the way dogs did, like they were about to pass out any minute and have a heart attack. He wanted to get her out, give her some proper air and check she really was OK, and that there wasn't a hole in her head.

He stopped to take the rucksack off and Jack immediately started to wind up her growl – and this time when he looked round, he saw the two men from the silver car weaving in and out between the trees. The big guy in the brown shirt, huffing and puffing, his big arms propped out like he was itching to do something with them; the skinny snapback doing his best to keep behind him. And Bully could scream and shout – but that was what kids did in a park, even big ones – so who was going to care?

03 07 10
DAYS HOURS MINUTES

He stopped thinking about that for a second when he heard the sound. The noise was incredible – like a plane going overhead, it came from above and shook the air. And though he heard it, he couldn't help but *listen* because it was the sound of a lion.

He veered towards the fence and caught sight of a penguin popping into a pool. A made-up jungle in the middle of London! He'd heard there was one but assumed it was miles away and not right bang *in* the middle. And there weren't just crappy cows here either, bused in from the countryside, but proper animals by the sounds of it. Stuff that could kill you; stuff that you wanted to *see*.

He started running, a sort of a hop and skip to jiggle Jack into the right place on his back. And then he swivelled, saw he had ten, maybe fifteen seconds to come up with something before the snapback caught up with him, grabbed him, slowed him right down for the big one to push around. He heard the brown shirt say, "Just *shove* him over! Get him on the ground."

ZOO EXIT flashed up on Bully's radar. He read the sign, understood it back to front – not as a *word* but as a way *in*, as a *ZOO ENTRANCE*. And he turned left sharp, wincing with the pain, ran past a staff girl in a green T-shirt with a camera at her face, snapping a family in a fake jungle. He cut in through the gift shop, pulled down a rack of cuddly giraffes and camels and then heard bigger crashes behind him. Then he was out, running past the penguins barking at Jack (Jack in the rucksack, giving it back). And people looking round as if to say: *Did that rucksack just* bark?

He ran on. Glimpses of animals inside their cages was all he was getting. Past the parrots and hippos, he ducked into the *Bugs Arena*, ran through a dark glass corridor full of big, bright little things painted green and yellow.

Out the other side, he took a narrow turn and was suddenly caught up in the queue funnelling into the monkey house.

He tried to slot in between the families but couldn't help pushing. He could smell the food on them, what they'd been eating. Cheese-and-onion crisps, ice creams, hot dogs … tiny bits of them going up his nose. It was no good though. Too slow this way. *Tut, tut, tut,* he heard, like some kind of bird, as he made his way through, but the queue had thickened up into a crowd. And there was nowhere left to push.

He turned round to go back but there was the brown shirt, his gut trying to get out of his jeans, the face above it all twisted up and out of breath. He met Bully's look from ten metres off, locked on like a fighter pilot with a red button to press, and Bully made up his mind to scream anyway.

He drew in the breath but held it, saw something the big guy wasn't seeing… A lot of green T-shirts.

"Excuse me, sir? Excuse me? Can I see your ticket?"

"What? Oh, I lost it, didn't I?"

The zookeeper wasn't taking that, her mouth set in a hard-to-please smile, another four T-shirts backing her up.

"Well, I need you to accompany me back then, please, sir, to the entrance. Please, *sir.*"

"Look… Look, love… I'm… I'm looking for my *kid.*"

He turned back to point Bully out. "He's over there somewhere!" he said because Bully had ducked down, was hiding out among the shoelaces and the pram wheels and the little kids. He shuffled along with the queue like that, like a creature looking for something to eat, and the next time he chanced a look, the big guy was swarming with green T-shirts, throwing wild, roundhouse punches, trying to wade on through them... He knocked one of them out and just as it looked as if he *might* break free, they got hold of his arms and legs and pulled him down.

15

03 **05** **56**
DAYS HOURS MINUTES

Bully was in the monkey house, winding his way through. And despite the situation he was enjoying himself because the monkeys – he couldn't get over it – the monkeys were allowed *out*. They were in the trees and on the benches, and the little kids around him were squealing and not believing it either.

One monkey landed on his rucksack, jumping straight off again when it felt jaws snapping underneath.

"Daddy! Look, Daddy! A doggy," said a girl.

"What, darling? Where?" asked the daddy, not seeing any doggy even when his daughter pointed to the long-haired girl – or was it a boy – with a rucksack, wearing cut-offs and flip-flops.

In a quiet spot outside, Bully went to one of the bins and hooked out an ice cream, good as new after a bite and quicker and cheaper than buying one from the shop. He saw a map in there too, of the zoo, and fished it out. It showed you where all the animals lived.

That set him thinking about buying his own zoo. He'd buy the lot and probably get a discount and move them into his place. He'd have his monkeys not in the house but in his garden. And he would have the lions and tigers caged up during the day but they could wander about at night, helping out with security. And he would get a digger and dig a pond for the hippos and penguins and the big goldfish from Japan. And he would get giraffes and they could earn their keep too. He would train them to *fetch*. If he was upstairs and the postman delivered his dog magazines then they could just pick them up and poke their heads through his bedroom window.

Maybe he'd get rid of the hyenas, he thought, looking at the pictures. He remembered from a nature programme how they laughed just the way Man Sammy had done, making fun of him when he'd said about his numbers coming up. And no snakes. And he didn't fancy having vultures on the roof either, thinking he was dead if he overslept and pecking his eyes out.

He only wanted good animals, not the sneaky, creepy ones. And then he thought about who was going to have to feed them and look after them and all the mess they would make in his new house and garden. And finishing off his ice cream, he thought perhaps it might be easier to just save his money (like he had with his ice cream) and come back and see everything here at this zoo another day.

Because it was time to go and the zoo was getting on for closing up. The crowds had thinned out, and it was just him and the camel over there, looking ready to spit. And right next to him, on the other side of a fence, something that looked like an Afghan hound crossed with a feather duster. It just had claws instead of paws and its nose was half as long as the rest of it put together. He could see a baby one shuffling about in a burrow under a special see-through hill. And this baby one was looking at him, up on its hind legs. It was no dog, that was for sure, but it reminded him of Jack when he'd found her under that 4x4.

He looked to see what it was on his map. It was called an *Anteater*. And from his map he could see that they were at the far end of the zoo. At the other end, next to the birdcage, was a little *n* for north and another exit. And he saw when he got out of the zoo that his next steps would be *off* the map, back into the white paper of London.

He folded up his map and set off towards the north exit, through the tunnel and past the giraffes and the hyenas and hunting dogs, and when he heard Jack growl, he didn't bother looking round because of the dogs. But if he had, he'd have seen a red snapback shadowing him, texting on his mobile phone.

03 **02** **35**
DAYS HOURS MINUTES

The sky was running out of sun but it was still bright to his left, to the west, as he headed a rough north, following the little arrow clenched in his hand. He kept away from the long main roads now, with the evening traffic building up even on a Sunday, and walked down the side streets.

When the road began to go uphill he thought that was good because it felt like he was going *up* north. He was pretty sure now that when he got out of London, things would get better and he would find someone to cash in his ticket for him.

Hampstead it said when he finally got to the top of a very long hill. And he squinted hard and looked down to where he had been but he could not see the zoo, or the Eye, blinking out the end of the day, not even a thin strip of brown river.

It was a posh kind of place full of one-off shops with names he hadn't seen before. He planned to push on but when he saw the newsagent's outside the tube station he couldn't resist it – he got his fiver out and went in and bought two cans of Coke – one for him, one for Jack.

"Uh-oh, what's that?" said the till lady when he'd bought the drinks and turned round to leave. And Bully didn't bother telling her what she was *uh-ohing* at.

Outside, he drank his can down in one. As he glugged, he clocked four boys, older than him, ganged up across the road. They kept looking at their phones, and then looking up as if waiting for someone specific to arrive, waiting – he realized – for *him*. He felt sick and panic sent his skin buzzing.

Slowly he began to walk away, keeping his eyes to the ground (if you looked at them, they looked at you). Then his head went back without his say-so and all he could see was the dark blue sky.

"You busted my car! You little—"

Bully half swivelled round, saw the red snapback right in his face; grey, gappy teeth in ones and twos, spitting out swear words at him.

Bully twisted away, tried to punch his way out of trouble, but the snapback was hanging on to his hair and the smooth soles of the flip-flops weren't giving him any grip. He kicked them off but he couldn't get away and the skinny guy in the snapback was starting to yell out. All the zombies did was stand and watch like it was on TV. And as he spun round Bully caught a look at the boys across the road, wising up to what was going down.

Snap!

The snapback had been snapped at! He was yelling and screaming his head off, with Jack's teeth poking out of the flap, giving him a proper munch. See how that felt!

"Drop it!" Bully commanded, because though the guy wasn't much heavier than him, he was *towing* him. And then Jack stopped mincing his arm up, let go and Bully was gaining speed and running into the underground.

There were no staff about and he forced his way through the barriers. He looked for the escalators but there was just a big square lift the size of his old blue bedroom.

He ran into it, looking for the buttons to press, but there were no buttons and the doors weren't shutting either. The faces were looking at him, then seeing Jack, blood on her fangs, and they were shrinking back against the metal walls … didn't want to share a lift with *that*.

He could see back through the barriers that the boys were

across the road now and there was no way the lift doors were going to close before they got to him.

He wanted to stay where he was. That same feeling he got every day but ten times worse in the lift. And he had to fight it. He had to fight it *now*; didn't have all day, just a few seconds more to make his mind up. Was he going or staying?

"That dog really should be on a lead..." a woman's voice inside the lift was saying, her voice floating about outside his head. And he got out the lift, got ready to run back through the barriers and sprint as hard as he could and maybe, maybe ram through the boys.

And then he saw the stairs.

EMERGENCY STAIRS
This stairway has over 320 steps.
Do not use except in case of an emergency...

Well, this *was* one.

The steps didn't just go straight down, they went round and round in a spiral like water going down a plughole. He took them two, three at time, grasping at the metal banister. Round and round, down and down he went. The yellow metal edges of the stairs blurred into one long golden path. The rucksack was cutting into his waist, really hurting him now, jolting and making him scream in his mouth, but he didn't have time to get Jack out and he tunnelled on through the pain, down and down and down...

He could hear feet behind him, catching him up – but

just one or two sets – where were the other feet? They were taking the lift, that's what they were doing – outflanking him – and his heart got ahead of him for a second because he had no way out if they got to the platform first. Still, though, he carried on running, trying to gauge how fast a lift could travel. He could hear the feet behind him, thumping on the metal strips … *bang, bang, bang* … didn't look round, just kept going on down… How many steps was it now? A hundred? Less? More? How quick was a lift? What would he do when he got to the bottom? It was the sort of maths they didn't teach you at school.

Then he nearly had a heart attack – feet were coming *up* the stairs – and he put on his own brakes but it was just a man – a weekend zombie, head down, a coffee in one hand, tired of waiting for the next lift. And as Bully went past him he took advantage of the situation and deployed *defensive counter-measures* and flicked the cup of coffee all over the man so that he took up the whole stairs, complaining and shouting about it. That should slow them down.

A breeze pushed past him. He matched that up to what he knew: a train coming in, the sound rushing after it, brakes squealing.

As he sped up again he ignored the voice in his head telling him his legs were giving out, because he could see the brighter lights of the platform now – and he came pelting down onto it, voices echoing fifty or sixty steps behind.

Mind the gap, mind the gap, said the platform announcer. *Get in the train, get in the train,* said the voice inside Bully's head. And further down the platform he heard the lift doors opening… *Beep, beep, beep.*

"There! There! Get 'im! Get 'im!" Jackals and vultures came screeching and swooping down the platform towards him, and with the train doors beginning to narrow and not caring about the gap, he turned sideways and flung himself through.

Seconds later, double faces at the glass, spitting, mouthing terrible things, just millimetres between the words and Bully as the tube train pulled away.

03 **01** **58**
DAYS HOURS MINUTES

Bully looked at the tube map above his head. He was on a straight *black* line, the *Northern* line. This was good. If he stayed on the tube the whole way to the end of the line then Watford couldn't be far. And there was Brent Cross! He could stop off there and go looking for Tiggs and Chris. They would help him out.

The train was pulling into the next stop but instead of Golders Green it said Belsize Park and Bully saw the train was travelling back into town, going south. It was the *wrong* stop, and the *wrong* way.

03 **01** **57**
DAYS HOURS MINUTES

And now he was waiting on an empty platform on the opposite track, waiting for the next train, back *north*. Only the platform wasn't empty now. And he was trying to pretend to himself that he hadn't heard the feet squeaking out of the train ten carriages back, and trying to convince himself that none of the boys had jumped onto one of the other carriages nearer the lift. He wasn't looking. He was *refusing* to look. For this minute his head had had enough of looking out for fear, and his lungs were full to the brim with it. He had lost his edge.

03 **01** **56**
DAYS HOURS MINUTES

He looked down the tunnel instead, begging for the train to come in. And he shuffled his toes onto the yellow line of the platform, squinted into the darkness for the smallest speck of light. But there was no train coming in, just humans *moving in* on him, to his left, at the edges of his vision, where he was choosing not to stare.

"Give us the ticket!" the boy said in an almost cheerful whisper, couldn't believe his luck. And then Bully *had* to look. There were two boys, bigger than him. One black, one white.

Bully held his penknife up. It wasn't much of a weapon, especially with the blades still inside. They cackled at it, like Man Sammy had. The fun was over now and they were shouting, threatening, trying to work themselves up to rush him, to get it out of him before the next train came in. They were taking their time, though, because neither one was a leader – the alpha dog (he'd read about them in his magazines). Every pack has an alpha and these boys were the tag alongs, the beta dogs. But that didn't mean they *weren't* going to go for him.

And then a shiver went through him, but a good one that made him feel full of himself, pushing the fear out of him, out of his chest and into the tunnel. And he smiled, he really did smile, when he remembered that he had *another* weapon, better than any penknife.

It threw them when he knelt down, kept them back just long enough for Bully to say, "Here! Jack! Here, girl! OUT!" And she couldn't *wait* to get out! And when they saw that dog with a head full of shark's teeth, blood bubbling between her ears, they were breathing in Bully's fear. He could almost see it, like it was a mist.

"Back off!" said Bully. "Back off. You're not getting nothing!" And they did, they backed away, swearing and threatening, but they did back away up the steps.

The train whistled in. Bully jumped on with Jack. The boys heard the doors beeping and ran for the exit, back up to the street for a signal for their phones to tell the rest of the gang he was travelling back the way he'd come.

03 01 51
DAYS HOURS MINUTES

That was their mistake, because Bully did a brave thing, his head telling him this was the best thing to do but his heart having nothing to do with it. He went and jumped *off* the train as soon as their ankles were starting to disappear up the steps.

Never get predictable.

So, he was being unpredictable now. Not doing what he wanted to do, which was get on this train. He looked up at the information board and saw it change and lose a minute of his life, of his ticket's life, as he thought about what to do next.

03 **01** **39**
DAYS HOURS MINUTES

He took a long time getting out of the station, willing himself to leave. He was confused and couldn't understand how they were getting *ahead* of him, waiting for him now, not even chasing along after him. And then when he'd got safely away from the tube station, he did a little angry dance. He'd told the Sammies he was going north, to Camelot, hadn't he? So they knew where he was going, they were taking short cuts, getting ahead of the game like the wolf in the fairy tale.

He blinked. His eyes were stinging with the salt that had dried and crusted into the corners. He spat on his fingers and rubbed them until they itched. Then he rubbed them some more. He knew it made it worse but he carried on doing it. He got his compass out. A little bubble of air trapped inside came to the surface of the glass as he watched the arrow inside slowly turn to find its way.

He stopped walking. And he really thought about what he was doing, about the boys and men now maybe further up the road, higher up, waiting for him, and he tried to think how they would think. *Getting to know his enemy.* They would be expecting him, just like a kid, to carry on up the road, carry on heading to Camelot to get his money. Then he had a moment of clarity, how to turn this thing on its head and let them spend all night chasing his shadow while he stayed put until the morning. It would lose him time but he might get to keep his ticket.

He left the main road through the town and crossed a park. He needed a place indoors: a place that never closed, where you didn't have to buy anything. Somewhere they let *anybody* in, even someone like him without any shoes.

He found this sort of place on a quiet road. It was called the *Royal Free Hospital*. Well, that sounded good to him, and though it didn't look anything like Buckingham Palace it was definitely *free*. The sign said so. Also, he might find someone to cash in his ticket for him. Someone old or, better still, on their way out, who didn't have much time left, like him. Because three days was all he had now.

They didn't let you take dogs into hospital though. There wasn't a sign but he just had this feeling, so he kept Jack in the rucksack and told her to be quiet and walked on in through the revolving doors, pushing too hard and having to wait for them to catch up and let him through. He walked past two nurses dealing with people just walking in like him who didn't seem any more hurt than he was.

He went to the café place. It was closed up on a Sunday night, and the shutters were down. There was a vending machine along the corridor but he'd dropped his change on the hill. He looked up and down the white hallway.

And then quickly, with his rucksack hiding what he was doing, he bent down and put his arm in through the slot and shoved it up as high as he could but he couldn't quite reach the chocolate.

When he pulled his hand back out, it was stuck on the metal lip of the lid. He yanked it but it only hurt more, and in frustration, he barged the machine. The alarm went off, his arm came out grazed and bleeding.

He took the stairs to get away, passing a doctor coming down, who saw his empty feet but carried on going. No one seemed bothered that he had no shoes in here. He understood why on the next floor when he pushed through some double doors and an old lady in bare feet with a balloon full of water shuffled towards him. Even though the corridor was plenty wide enough he got out the way. She looked like she had her bed dress on back to front, and he was horrified when he saw her bare old bum following along after her.

He decided to go up another floor. And when he came out of the doors there was a trolley with a few empty dinner plates waiting to be taken down in the lift. He picked out a spud and a sausage. He forced himself to feed the sausage to Jack and wondered if there was more where that came from. He went to the end of the corridor to take a look.

Blarrr, blarrr, blarrr!

His head filled up with an alarm much worse than the little *shriek, shriek* of the vending machine and he assumed he'd set it off, whatever it was, by nicking half a sausage. He put his hands to his ears to keep any more of the *blarrr,*

blarrr from getting in while he tried to run away from it.

Then nurses started leaping out of rooms and coming down corridors as if they'd been hiding there all day, just waiting for this. But they ran past him and he heard them yelling *"Crash! Crash! Crash!"* and he saw it was nothing to do with him.

Two doctors were coming now, pushing a heart start trolley really fast towards him. To avoid them he went round the corner, spied a door with a little window and, thinking it was a store cupboard, he was already in it before he saw the man in the bed.

03 01 23
DAYS HOURS MINUTES

"Now *where* have *you* been?" An old Davey was lying on the bed, staring right at him. "Now *where* have *you* been?" He said it again like he was asking him and not giving him a telling-off. Bully just stood there, not wanting to say.

"Come in then, come in." He waved his withery hand. He looked as good as dead but then all Daveys did.

"Shut the door, shut the door. On your back, the thing … the thing, that bag on your back. With the *sack*," he said, still waving his arm, the skin hanging down and flipping about like it might slip off his bone. "That's a rucksack! Now *where* have *you* been?"

"The zoo," Bully said because that had been the best part of his day so far.

"Oh, the *zoo*…" The old man's face relaxed, like he'd taken a big swig of something good. "What did you see?"

Bully looked round again, checking the door. The nurses and doctors were still shouting at each other.

"Now *where* have *you* been?"

"I said. The zoo."

Jack began to whimper, the bit of sausage had started up her guts because it was well gone her teatime.

"Shh," said Bully.

"What's that? What have you got there, in your sack? A penguin? What is it that you've got there?"

Bully sniggered. "Nah!" he said. "It's a dog."

Bully wasn't scared of this Davey, even if he was dying, saying things like did he have a penguin in his bag.

"Oh. A dog." The man's face lit up and his eyes stopped wandering. And instead of asking if it was *his* dog, he said, "Well, let's have a look at him then! Get him out, get him out."

Bully put the rucksack on the ground and got Jack out. He winced with the pain, the skin raw on his hips.

"Oh, is that a Staffy?" said the Davey and now it was Bully's turn to smile because this Davey knew at least one thing about dogs.

"Yeah, yeah. She's a Staff cross. She's crossed with something really good, a real proper breed with a pedigree and everything."

"Oh, what does that matter? What's her name? That's all that matters. Having a good name. That's all that matters. What's her name?"

"Jack. She's Jack."

"Oh… Jack! That is a *good* name. I know someone called Jack. Who is it?" he said.

He was mad, this Davey, but he was all right, Bully decided, as long as he stayed where he was. Bully sniffed the tray at the end of the bed and the man caught him looking as he hoped he would.

"Are you hungry?"

"Yeah."

The man looked around the little room helplessly. "Sometimes they leave things to eat."

"That." Bully pointed to the dinner.

"Oh, what is it?"

"Food."

"Oh, yes, you can eat that."

Bully took the lid off and it was shepherd's pie. His mum used to make it and Phil used to say it had real shepherd in it to put him off.

He took a big spoonful and then another two and then put the plate on the floor for Jack to finish.

"Finish it all, finish it all," said the Davey when he saw Bully looking at the custard dessert. Bully finished it and pocketed the metal spoon because he had lost that too in his coat, along with the last little bit of his mum in the card.

"I'm private and this is *my* room with a view," the Davey said and pointed to the window. The darkness outside was beginning to reflect the light back into the room and Bully could see nothing out there, just the road and a few trees.

He checked the door again, put his face right up to the glass. Things were getting calmer now, one of the nurses shaking her head, another one nodding. He looked at the old man. He thought he would be polite and ask how long he'd been here and what was wrong with him, like you did when you came to visit people in hospital.

"You been here long?"

"I don't know. I don't think so. I don't know. Do you?" he asked hopefully.

Bully shrugged. "You had a bit of a kickin' or sumin'?"

"No, no," said the man and Bully nodded because his face didn't look too bad, not bashed about. Just those spiders up his nose, and red and blue lines all over his cheeks, like a little kid had been colouring him in while he was asleep.

"I'm going home tomorrow."

"Yeah?"

"Yes. I'm going home…"

"You ever been to Watford, mate?" The question came out before he thought about it.

"Oh, Watford. I don't know. I'd *love* to go."

"You got a car then?"

"Oh, yes. I do. I'm sure I have. I have a car somewhere out there. A silver one," he said and it reminded Bully of the men who'd been following him. A car was good news. A car was luxury. A car was a flat on wheels; somewhere to sleep, to eat, somewhere to get you someplace. Back on his estate you had to wait to go anywhere, for a bus or a lift into town. A car would get him out of here straight away.

Bully took a big breath. "Could you do me a favour, mate?"

"What? What?"

"I've got this ticket, yeah?"

"A ticket? Yes?" He was staring at Bully but as if he were further back in the room.

"Yeah, but I need someone to collect on it. It's a secret though. And gangstas are trying to rob me. *I* bought it for *my mum* and *she* gave it back to *me* for my birthday because she was dying." He thought it best to get that straight. "But I'm too young to play, so it's got to be someone older than me who has to go and get the money from Camelot in Watford. And then you go and give it back to me. It's got to be that way. I'll give you some of it but you'd have to give me all of it first, you get me?"

"What?"

"The money," said Bully. "What I won."

"Bit of luck on the gee-gees?"

"The what? No." This guy wasn't understanding straight. So Bully told him a bit more of the story, filled him in so that it sounded like something believable, something real instead of just a story a kid with a dog was telling him to cheer him up in hospital. It took a while with the bloke nodding him along, then pointing out the window, going on about his private view of the darkening road and the trees.

Finally Bully stopped talking. He could see the Davey was thinking it over. Bully had decided he wasn't going to give him anything like half. He could have *half* a million instead. That would do him for what he had left to live.

He checked the little window in the door. No one was rushing about any more. And when he squinted sideways there was just one nurse over at the desk.

He looked back. Jack was up on the bed and the old man was patting her and crying, his eyes like little yellow fried eggs. That frightened Bully because he was smiling at the same time. He picked up the rucksack, nervous and wanting to get when this Davey was going to take him to Watford sorted out.

The man looked at him and stopped crying. He didn't rub his face dry but instead just looked surprised.

"Now *where* have *you* been?" he asked in the same voice as he'd done a Scooby-Doo ago.

03 **01** **03**
DAYS HOURS MINUTES

Bully was going to sleep in the hospital but a security guard found him on the stairs and started asking him why he was there. And by the time he got out of the hospital the sky was more black than blue.

He didn't feel safe out in the open any more among the late-night dog walkers, dogs off the lead and sniffing round his rucksack. So when he came to a high wall, he went over it. The top had spikes curling above it like old, dead fingers but he just grabbed them and heaved himself over. Even with the rucksack on it wasn't hard because he was mostly skin and bone.

The first thing he saw was a lump of stone stuck in the ground, and another, and another, with angels poking out all over the place. He was in a grave place, a cemetery. And this, he thought, was a good place to hide out – just like the hospital, anyone could go there but nobody really wanted to. He felt like running back and telling the Davey in the hospital that this was where he was going to end up; that this was going to be his view very soon. He wanted to get back at him for what he'd done, getting Bully's hopes up, playing tricks, making promises he didn't know how to keep.

He took Jack out of the rucksack, left it by a gravestone, and they went for a walk. Bully kept to the big wide paths and he stopped every so often to touch a name carved into a stone. As he wandered around in that last bit of extra light you got in summer time, he cheered himself up thinking that the people looking for him wouldn't be happy either.

They went past a few stone coffins that were empty, with their lid half off or smashed, like someone inside had had enough of being stuck in there. As he walked he kept sniffing, night green smells and old water sneaking in past his cold. And then he felt his feet getting *colder* and he looked down and saw he was walking on gravestones: a whole path of them leading off into the black green of bushes and trees.

He shivered, jumped back onto the grass and started seriously thinking about where he was going to sleep. There must be a toilet, some place somewhere. But when he tried to go back to the main path he was lost.

He got his compass out but that was no good because he hadn't checked which direction he'd been heading when he came over the wall. And as the bushes and the darkness thickened up around him, he thought he saw what looked like a little old-fashioned street full of little old pointy houses. But as he got closer he saw that these houses weren't for living in. No one had ever lived in them. They were for being *dead* in. And their huge iron and stone doors had only ever opened and closed once or twice for those inside. And now he was in among them, he saw they weren't so little.

They loomed above him, carving off that last little bit of light from the summer sky.

He stopped walking, saw a tunnel of these tombs winding into the darkness. He wasn't going any further down there…

And then that last speck of light in the sky was gone. And though the stars were out, they didn't shine this far down. He flicked his lighter on, but the darkness was still there, pushing up against him inside his little bubble of light.

He tried very hard not to look right and left, not to swing the lighter about, but when he did he caught more of the angels, the bad ones between the trees, dragging little kids to heaven. Another one pointing him out with white fingers, as if to say: *He's the one! He's the one with the winning ticket!* And there were more of them at his feet. Kipping just off the path, trying to trip him up!

"Where's the wall, mate? Where we going?" But Jack didn't seem to know either, she just whined like she was scared. And Bully had to listen to the sound of his own feet hurrying after them as he went down one path then another, his head going right and left until he stopped looking where he was going, and that was when he ran and tripped right in front of the hound crouched ready and waiting to rip his throat out.

"Hurrgh," he said, scrabbling back to his feet. But when the dog didn't go for him, didn't pounce – didn't even *breathe* – he reached out and touched it.

It was cold, stone cold, and part of a gravestone. And it wasn't waiting to rip his throat out but resting with its head between its paws, forever looking out for the poor bloke six feet under the ground. And he couldn't help being impressed. He didn't know you could put a whole dog on your grave. He wouldn't mind getting one of those for his gravestone when he'd spent his millions and he was dead, because he didn't want to end up like his mum as just ashes in a sweetie jar, dumped in a bin.

Then he heard an extra big noise like something *extra big* coming at him and he yelled and he was *off*, frantically clicking the flint on his lighter, *click, click, click.*

03 00 18
DAYS HOURS MINUTES

They came out over a different wall onto a lane on a hill. And he ran straight over to the nearest streetlamp to get his breath back. When he did, he found he was very thirsty because he hadn't taken any water at the hospital.

He walked on up the lane past a blue van that he gave the once over, considering breaking into it. *Highgate Plumbing and Solar* it said on the side. At the next row of houses he went looking in the back gardens for a water tap and maybe a shed to spend what was left of his night. He went from garden to garden, catching sight of someone in front of the TV, a long, long way away.

Jack chased a cat. Bully told her off; they were on manoeuvres and you didn't chase cats, you kept your head down.

Three gardens in from the lane he found a tap on the

outside wall of a house. There weren't any lights on inside, just a glow coming in from next door but he still ducked down as low as he could while he assessed the situation. And Jack was taking it more seriously, waiting, invisible in the long grass.

He turned the tap on as quietly as he could but it still squeaked when no water came out. He twisted it backwards and forwards and he felt like screaming and crying. And then he calmed down and thought about why there were no lights on and no water on in this house; why somebody might have turned the lights and the water *off*.

03 **00** **03**
DAYS HOURS MINUTES

He peered through the kitchen blinds into the darkness. He wondered how long they'd been gone for, weeks by the look of the grass and all the flowers in the pots, growing mad. He thought about picking one of the pots up and chucking it through the window but that would make a lot of noise, and that sort of smashing always woke everyone up on his estate. Then he remembered that people who lived in houses sometimes left keys outside, in case they couldn't get back in, and he went looking under the doormat and feeling round the window frame. He even lifted up all the pots to look underneath them with his lighter but there was no key.

It began to rain then, just wetting the air, nothing heavy, but he went and sat under the little porch, too tired to move off just yet. A dog next door started yapping. Something big and fluffy, he could tell. He warned Jack not to bark back and then he thought again about breaking in. He picked up the pot on the step under the porch. It didn't have anything much in it, just a couple of twigs like the pigeon had in its beak on the poster in crustie town.

Why did these people have all these flowers and plants in pots when they already had a garden? It made him angry again and he liked the feeling of it, taking the edge off just how tired he was.

He weighed the pot in his hand. He would chance it, throw it through the kitchen window and hope the neighbours were bad neighbours and wouldn't bother to come looking. He got ready, and then as an afterthought, he pulled the twigs off the pot and the whole lot came out, roots and everything. And just before he lobbed it, he heard a *clink* on the patio. He got down on his knees and saw what looked like little golden teeth shining in the dirt.

02 **23** **20**
DAYS **HOURS** **MINUTES**

When he unlocked the back door with the key he thought it was a squat for a minute. That he'd got it wrong. There was washing-up crusting in the sink and the bin stank worse than his bins and the kitchen was just a *mess*. But the electric was on when he opened the fridge and he left it that way for a bit of light.

Nothing much in there that he recognized as food. There was hard butter and some jars of funny-looking jam. The cupboards weren't much better. He found something in a yellow bottle called *cordial* and a loaf of dried-out bread. He thought the cordial might be wine but it just tasted sweet, and he drank it neat and then buttered the end of the stale loaf of bread under his arm, and ate it the way a rat might, gnawing at the end. Then he defrosted some meat for Jack. And while the microwave was whirring, he had a look round the rest of the house.

When he found the shutters were closed on the front windows he turned the lights on. He wasn't impressed. It was a right mess in here too: clothes draped on sofas and hanging off doors. The state of the place was bad. And all the walls were white like they'd just been given the keys to the place by the council, and there were no proper carpets anywhere. There were some paintings on the walls that brightened it up a bit but they were rubbish. The best one was a naked lady with lovely wavy hair stuck inside a big seashell, but the rest of them weren't of *anything*: worse than Cortnie used to do with her felt tips.

He fed Jack and then went upstairs. He flicked another light on. He had never climbed upstairs inside a house before. All the stairs between the floors in the tower block were on the outside. It was a strange feeling and he clung on to the banister that wound up the wooden hill like he was in a fairy tale, pictures of a mum, a dad and two kids on the wall. Lots of books upstairs, all different sizes and colours, one room just full of them, no bed or nothing, just books, a desk and a chair. Bully preferred magazines but he didn't *mind* books as long as they were interesting ones with real stuff in and not full of *stories*. What he didn't understand, though, was why people kept them for so long after they'd read them.

When Bully went into the first kid's room he could tell from the clothes and the sort of school books that the boy was older than him. He had a look in the wardrobe, kicked a few things about and then he saw a skateboard propped up in the corner. He took that and a laptop into the next room, the girl's room. The bed was messier than the boy's, clothes all over it, and he felt comfortable sleeping somewhere that didn't seem looked after. He lay down on the bed, Jack next to him, getting used to laying on beds now because she'd never been allowed to back at the flat.

Something else he couldn't work out ... spending all that money ... on books ... and not a single *telly* in the house. And as he began to drift off to sleep he tried to imagine a place where there was no TV in the bottom of a deep dark cave without electricity, because even in prison they gave you something to watch.

18

02 **09** **10**
DAYS HOURS MINUTES

For the second time in three days Bully woke up to find a girl staring at him. And though this one was older, just like his half-sister she screamed when she saw Jack.

Bully jumped up, fell off the bed. By the time he was on his feet the girl was gone and a man was in the doorway.

"What you doing here, boy?"

The man looked like someone he knew. He didn't know who. Then he realized that this was the man in the photo, the dad. He was still confused. He had a feeling that he'd slept through most of the day. Had *lost* a day. He was angry with himself. He was already *in* today and racing through it. It was like breaking into a note. Once you did that, it was as good as gone.

"I'm—" He was about to say *going* but experience had taught him it was always best to just *go* and he made a bolt for the door. The man surprised him by getting out his way, then shutting the door after him. Bully was halfway down the stairs before he realized Jack was still in the bedroom.

"Let 'er out!" He could hear Jack throwing herself at the door, pawing, barking, desperate.

176

"Why you here, boy? Tell me and I'll let it *out*."

Bully felt for his penknife without thinking about it, moving back up the stairs, anger boiling and rocking him about as if he were a cheap kettle.

"John! Just let him go, OK?" A woman downstairs – the mum – the girl next to her, long hair tied up in a messy knot.

Bully fumbled with the blade but he couldn't get it open because he'd ripped his nails the other night and the edge of the big blade was too greasy and wet.

"OK, don't be *silly*. Put that away, boy," the man said quietly, like he was trying to be a teacher. Bully, though, didn't like being called a boy.

"John, he's got a knife!" Bully looked back down and the mum and the boy were there now, the boy older *and* bigger than him, in jeans and a T-shirt, looking like his mum had bought him in a shop.

It was the girl, though, who began to move up the stairs. It unnerved him, that did, a girl coming towards him, and he waved his unopened knife at her as if to say no, he wasn't going to give it to her. And he retreated further, back towards the dad.

"Jo! Stay *there*, Jo. *Alex*, give me the phone!"

"My battery's gone!"

"Go and get the landline then!"

"Gimmie my dog back," said Bully. He was on the landing now, near enough to kick the man. "Give me my *effing* dog back *now*."

"Calm down, boy. Look, just *calm down*, boy," the man

said and Bully saw his fear and it scared him, like seeing a face suddenly flash up against a window. Bully looked down at his hand to see why the man was scared and now, magically, the blade was out. He couldn't remember doing it but he couldn't put it back now.

"Give *me*—" he said, but then his anger boiled dry and he felt hot and empty and he remembered for the hundredth time that he'd lost his mum's card and he'd never hear her voice again. His mouth twisted and something like a sneeze worked up behind his eyes and too late he realized he was going to cry.

02 08 06
DAYS HOURS MINUTES

After the man let Jack out and Bully stopped crying and Jack stopped snapping and barking and growling, the dad held out his hand. For the knife, Bully thought, but he went for the other hand, his right hand, to shake it.

"The name's *John*," he said in a quick, funny voice that sounded foreign. The way he said words was as if they meant something extra to him.

They sat him down with a cup of tea. Bully was starving. They let him put the sugar in, smiling a little wider with each spoonful. The mum was called Rosie. Bully thought she looked a bit old to be a mum, her hair running out of colour, the curls just hanging on at the ends. She said that they'd just got back from abroad, visiting some girl called *Siena* in Italy.

"Sorry," she said, looking around the kitchen. "Sorry it's such a *mess*. We left in a bit of rush." And he realized they were apologizing to him for the state of the place.

How old was he, they wanted to know. He lied automatically and said sixteen. The boy, Alex, sniffed, didn't think so. *Was he homeless?* He gave a nod, though he called it sleeping out. *How long?* He wouldn't tell them, didn't want them knowing how many days in case it was too many and they went and told the Feds. *What had happened to him?* He'd lost his spot, he said, and his shoes and his coat. He left out Janks and the dead man and said nothing about his numbers coming up. *Did he want to phone anyone, his mum and dad, to tell them he was OK?* He just shrugged at that one because it wasn't that he didn't want to, just that he couldn't.

The mum finished up by saying that he *must* stay for something to eat. He didn't say no and didn't say yes until they had him sat down at a table eating *risotto*. It looked like thick sick. Except for meaty burps, he'd never swallowed any sort of puke before, but it tasted the right side of cheesy. He finished it quick, to get going, but they kept asking him questions and talking. And he didn't know how they ever finished their food, all the talking they did. It was very tiring having to look up all the time when you were eating.

"You can stay the night, Bully, if you'd like to," the dad said while Alex, the boy, was stacking the plates up, and Bully could see his face go solid like what was left of the *risotto*.

Bully had heard the boy going on to his dad earlier: *I don't care what you say, Dad... He broke in ... totally wrecked Mum's lime tree ... and why was my skateboard in Jo's room? You can't trust him ... you should definitely get the police in, just in case he's done something...*

Bully didn't like him. Things he couldn't put into words – not just his size and strength or the clothes he wore, but the way he held himself, the way he moved about, as if he owned the place.

"Yeah, OK then," he said in the end about sleeping, because even though he had slept all day he was still very tired and heavy and his body ached, and it was better than some shed. And if he got up early he still had *two* days.

The mum ran him a bath and put clothes out and said she would wash his.

"It's just some stuff that doesn't fit Alex any more." It was a T-shirt and a coat that said *Superdry* on it and a pair of jeans and a pair of trainers, *Adidas* ones that were way too big until the mum got him some more socks to make them fit.

"They'll do you for now," she said.

"You can have 'em back," he said.

"No, no. They're yours to keep."

He didn't say anything, but when he got his winnings he'd get a pair of Reeboks. Box fresh. And more than just one pair. He'd get a pile of them, like they had in the shops. No, what he would do ... he'd *buy* the shop. He'd buy *all* the shops so he didn't have to go shopping. Either that or do it all on the internet.

The mum did his bath with bubbles in. Before he got in, he

caught himself in the big long mirror – this skinny kid, all the cuts and bruises – and it frightened him, like he was changing into someone else. And he was glad of the bubbles in the bath.

"You look like you've freshened up," the mum said when she saw him downstairs. "Are you OK?" His nose kept twitching with the smell around him coming and going because of his cold and he realized it was *him*, right under his nose, the clean clothes on his back. "Would you like something else to eat or anything to drink?" He shook his head but she was still staring at him, at his head. The rubber bands had snapped when the snapback yanked his ponytail and his hair was all over his face now.

"Is there anything I can do? What about – would you like me to tidy up your hair for you? Just the ends?"

"Mum," the girl said. "That's so *random.*"

"Why, what's wrong with that? I used to do yours when you were little – younger," she corrected, seeing Bully's face begin to fall.

"You never did Alex's!"

"Well, he was always fussier than you."

Bully liked that idea that Alex was fussy about his hair. Only girls were fussy about their hair. Phil used to shave his whenever it got too long, right down to nothing so that it looked like someone had dotted his head in full stops. His mum went mad every time Phil did it but he said he was only saving them money.

"His hair's cool like that, anyway. A lot of boys have it like that now, Mum."

"S'all right," Bully said. He liked this idea, that it was "cool" to have long hair, but he'd been thinking if she cut his hair and he wore his new clothes it would be like a disguise for getting *north*. So he nodded again. She got him to sit on a chair in the kitchen and put a towel round his neck and Jo sat at the table and watched, said she would make sure her mum didn't do anything too drastic.

The mum was right up in his face and he saw she wasn't pretty like his mum. She had wrinkles all the time, even when she wasn't talking, and her hair was *very* crinkly and her eyebrows looked like they were fighting for space on her face, but she talked to him nice, not like some people did to kids and dogs.

"When was the last time you had it cut then? If you don't mind me asking?" she asked him.

"Dunno," he said, though he did.

"Was it when you were at home?" He nodded, would go along with that.

"Is home a long way away?" He nodded. It was *miles* away.

"And do you want to go back?"

He shook his head and he heard a loud *snip*.

"Mum!" said Jo.

"It's all right. It's fine. Go and get me the mirror and I'll just even it up a bit…" She pulled a concentrating face for a minute, and the wrinkles started joining up, and then she asked, "Why don't you want to go home? Is it something you can tell me?"

"No," he said, not wanting to shake his head in case she

cut his ear off. And it wasn't something he could tell her. It would take a lot of haircuts to do that. Not to explain everything – that would take just a few snips – but to let himself do the telling – that would take a while.

Jack let out a short sharp bark, jealous of all this attention Bully was getting.

"Oi, shut it," he said. Jack sat back down, her bowed front legs still slightly raised, as if to catch any affection that might fall her way.

"He's well trained, isn't he?" the mum said and Bully felt his heart go, and he wanted to tell her then, surprising himself. But the girl, back with the mirror, started talking.

"I didn't mean to scream earlier on. It was just that your dog – he looked a bit scary. What's he called?"

"Jack. He's not a he dog, though," he confided, seeing as she was a girl herself. "She's a she dog, a bitch."

"Oh, right," she said, laughing like people did, who didn't know about dogs and thought it was just rude to call a girl a bitch.

"So why did you call her Jack then?" asked the mum.

"I dunno," he said, though he did.

"So, what sort of dog is Jack then? A pit bull?" said the girl.

He couldn't speak. He was shocked by what she'd said.

"She's not a *pit bull*. She's *nothing* like a pit bull. She's a Staffy, a Staffy cross!"

"Oh right, sorry. I don't know much about dogs. Those kind of dogs all look sort of the same to me, but yours is really *nice*," she said. And that just about saved her in his eyes. And then the mum said of course not, of course Jack wasn't the *same* as any other dog. And what a lovely dog she was, and they didn't say anything more about different breeds after that.

They had a TV after all. And Bully was amazed at just how small and old and fat it was. He wasn't surprised they hid it in a cupboard. He would be embarrassed too if he had a TV like that.

The news came on. London. A shot of the guns and the war museum made his eyes go wide.

"That's the Imperial War Museum," said Alex. The interviewer man with the microphone was standing in the park giving an update. He didn't say anything about Janks, just an *unidentified male* killed some time between Saturday night and early Sunday morning. The news finished without anyone really noticing because of all the talking they were doing, the whole family. They all talked. The mum was the worst, words Bully couldn't even say, let alone understand.

"Shut up, Dad," said Jo when he complained about her changing channels. Bully looked to see if this might earn her a back-hander but it didn't.

"Where would you like to sleep tonight?" the mum asked him when the TV went *off.* "There's the spare bedroom in the loft but it's a bit of a mess up there, or you can sleep on the sofa if you like. It's up to you."

"Down 'ere then," he said. He could maybe put the tiny TV back on. Better than nothing.

"Jo, go upstairs to the attic and get the sleeping bag, will you?"

"D'you want to come up?" Jo said, turning back to him on the stairs. And he didn't say anything but followed her up.

The attic place was right at the top, above all the ceilings. The room had a slanting roof so that you couldn't stand up in the corners, which was just as well because it was full of stuff: more books, bags, clothes, like a charity shop that never sold anything.

She started searching for the sleeping bag. "When it's clear you can just about see St Paul's from here." He nodded, didn't know what she was going on about.

"Mum says it's the only place she'd ever get married, so I think Dad's safe. They're kind of old hippies."

Hippies. They didn't look like hippies. He pulled a look, didn't approve of crusties or hippies of any age – didn't realize the look was on his face until she said, "They're all right though."

"Your dad talks funny," said Bully.

"Oh yeah, he's still got an accent, hasn't he? He's from South Africa originally. He came over years ago when he met Mum."

"He dudn't look black," said Bully and Jo laughed until she saw he was being serious.

"No, not really… Anyway, there's the Eye, you can just about see it." And then he looked out because he knew what that was. He could just about still see it, like a glowing dot. About the same size as his eye, blinking out the end of the day. "And that's Highgate cemetery over there." She pointed to one of the little stone houses he'd seen the night before, across the lane. "Lots of famous people are buried there, like Karl Marx and George Eliot … and loads of *other* people too," she said when she saw he wasn't nodding to any of them. "They do guided tours if you want to look round."

"What? You have to *pay*?" He'd seen it for free last night, hadn't thought much of it either, at first, until he found the hound on the gravestone.

"Um, yes. I think it's about eight pounds. I suppose that's quite a lot really," she said, realizing eight pounds wasn't so cheap when you didn't have shoes. "I think the church is free though… Sorry, I don't know why I said that." When he looked at her, her cheeks were red like she'd put make-up on without him seeing. "I mean, anyone can just go in there. And sometimes people get you help and stuff. I'm not saying *you* need help. I just mean they're like safe places to go, sort of like sanctuaries, aren't they? Sorry, I'll shut up…"

She turned away and went back to searching for the sleeping bag but he knew what she meant: like a bird sanctuary. He'd been to one of those once and got a free pen. He realized he was still looking at her, just the back of her head, and he felt the same make-up on his face, turning it red. She was older than him. And everything.

"Here it is." She turned back to him, smiling like her mum did, just for the sake of it.

"Are you sure you don't want to sleep up here, instead?"

"Nah," he said. He was used to the couch.

An hour or so later, when everyone else had gone to bed, he lay awake thinking about what had happened to him in the last few days since he'd won the lottery. It was like watching a boy in a film – he didn't really think much about how this boy was feeling, what he was going through, he just wanted everything to be OK at the end. He kept watching it, over and over in his head, rewinding it each time he got to where he was now and wondering what was going to happen next, because the bit he was in *now*, in this house with these people, with all the stairs and books, felt like a trailer for another story.

19

01 **18** **07**
DAYS HOURS MINUTES

He woke up early with a plan that was *perfect*. He hadn't thought it up; it was just there when his eyes opened. As if someone had pulled back a curtain in his brain and let the light in. He didn't have to *look* sixteen; he just had to *prove* it. So what he needed to do was borrow someone else's proof and make it his. It needed to be an older boy and Alex was an older boy. Alex had a passport; they all did. He'd seen the mum putting them in the kitchen drawer next to the sink. And checking it was still quiet, and telling Jack to *stay*, he got off the couch. His foot felt better, almost perfect, and he worked his way around the edge of the room on tiptoe so the floorboards didn't squeak.

He found Jo's passport first. She was really called *Josephine* and that was much longer than Jo and he wasn't sure he liked it. He stared at the picture instead. This Josephine didn't really look like her either. She was years younger with a white, blank face trying to hide a grin and short hair just sitting on her ears, not doing anything. He flicked through the others and found the boy's passport. His real name was longer too. It was *Alexander*. Bully was glad about that though, because it was like Alex was pretending to be someone he wasn't. So it didn't matter if Bully robbed his passport and did the same thing.

He reckoned with the short blade of his knife he could slit the plastic and slide a photo of himself over Alex's picture. He'd get one from a photo cabin at a bus station or in a shopping centre and then *literally* wipe that smile off his face.

And if he ticked no publicity, Alex would never find out, no one would. Would Alex miss the passport, though? Bully didn't think so. Not until they went away next year, anyway. He thought about letting himself out and going with Jack but that would look suspicious so he decided to wait until everyone got up, wasting a few more hours of his ticket's life.

01 **14** **40**
DAYS **HOURS** **MINUTES**

He woke up again to see his cut-off shorts, hoodie and T-shirt on the arm of the couch. The mum had washed them and they were all dry, and white where the dirt had been rinsed out. He decided he liked his new clothes and left the old ones where they were. In the pocket of his new jeans he found a key – the key to the back door he'd used to get in. And though there was a very simple explanation as to *how* it got there, he didn't know *why* it was there. Why was Rosie giving him back the key to their house? He couldn't work it out.

He could hear voices in the kitchen, official voices talking. He thought it was the Feds, but after listening for a while he realized the voices were coming from a radio and he listened in case there was any more about the dead man in the park. Then the mum and dad started talking, talking about money – about it not stretching. And it would have to be camping in Wales next year. And Bully was pleased about that because he was pretty sure you didn't need a passport to go there.

All the concentrating and the listening was making him hungry so he went into the kitchen. They were reading papers, sitting at the table. The dad was dressed in blue overalls like he was fixing something. In the light Bully saw how white his hair was and how brown his head was. When they saw him, they smiled as if he was supposed to be there.

"Sorry, did we wake you up? Did you sleep well?" asked the mum. "Let me get you some breakfast." Bully shook his head but she seemed to know that he didn't mean it and got him some cereal and some milk.

"Can I drop you anywhere? John's off in a minute but I'm here all day."

The dad laughed. "Some of us have to go to work."

"Hey, I *earn* my holidays."

"Rosie's a teacher," the dad explained.

Bully was both fascinated and appalled that a real-life lady with a first name and everything could be a teacher. He could not imagine them existing outside the school gates. He imagined them more like, well, like zombies, just wandering around the classrooms all night on the lookout for leftover kids, because they were always there before him, first thing in the morning, going mad about being on time.

"I teach English, for my sins," she said, like it was *her* suffering the punishment.

Well, that explained *a lot* of the talking this family did. Out of all the teachers, the English ones went on and on more than all the others: about letters and dots and dashes and *words* and what they *meant*, as if they were teaching you a foreign language or something. And books. They went on and on about what books were about. Sometimes weeks after you had read them.

"And I'm a plumber," said the dad. A plumber, thought Bully, living in a house like this. That didn't add up. It wasn't right. Plumbers earned good money but they didn't live in houses full of books.

"Is that your van then?" asked Bully. "The blue one out on the road?"

"The old *heap*? Yep. That's mine and if it doesn't start I'll be getting you to give me a *push*." He stood up. He wasn't much bigger than Bully but that didn't seem to bother him. He came over to Bully and patted him on the back. "Only joking, *boy*. You have a good day, son. See you later maybe."

Jo came downstairs. Bully had hoped she would. Her hair was up on top of her head like a fancy bun today and she was still in her dressing gown and pyjamas.

Jack began to whine.

"Oi," he said. But she was hungry, wasn't she? Jo had gone

out and bought a small tin of dog food yesterday but it was gone now.

"Is she hungry? There's a shop at the top of the lane, in the square."

There was *thump, thumping* on the stairs. Alex came into the kitchen, avoiding Bully's eye.

"Morning, Alex," the mum said and then Bully saw her reaching for the drawer where the passports were.

"I got to go now," Bully said.

"OK … well, Jo, you get dressed and take Bully up to the shops and—"

"No, I got to go *now*."

"OK." She offered him her hand, money in it, and he took it.

Rosie showed him to the door and handed him his new coat, which he took, and the new trainers, which he put on. They were still too sloppy but they looked good.

"Oh, do you think you could do me a *really* big favour and bring back a loaf of bread? Just drop it off, if you're not stopping. Brown if they've got it. But it doesn't matter. Anything will do."

She opened the door for him and pointed up the hill. "Just straight up there. Go right to the top of Swain's Lane and you can see it across the square. Let me get you a bag."

He stepped back inside and caught Alex saying to Jo: "Yeah, right. He's coming back with the change…"

And Bully was really glad then that he had taken this *Alexander* boy's passport.

A few of the zombies were out and about but Bully felt good. He didn't mind them as he walked up to the shop. He was warm and dry and the sky was too. For the first time perhaps, he felt a bit like one of them. Places to go, things to do.

The shop was just where the mum had said it was. He looked around, scouted it first, a little wary, but he was sure now anyone looking for him would be in Watford, waiting for him there. He tried not to think about that as he tied Jack to a bollard outside the shop and went in. Sometimes if he had money, like now, he would take Jack in just to wind them up, but he didn't want to do that today.

They didn't have any tins with a Jack Russell on the label so he had to make do with one with an Alsatian instead. He was about to pay when he remembered the bread; brown she'd said, and he chose the brownest-looking bread he could find, which took some time, comparing all the loaves.

The man at the till smiled at him.

"Put that on toast, eh?" he said, nodding at the dog food. It was only after Bully left the shop that he realized that this was a joke.

Outside the shop someone slapped him on the back, hard. He twitched forward onto his toes, pulling away, already off and running in his head.

"Heh, heh! Slow down, man. Where you been?"

It was Chris. He looked shorter and fatter with his pirate rag on his head, like someone had stood on him and only

193

just taken their foot off, and he had a bit of a beard, just fuzzy stuff, so it took Bully a second to recognize him.

"I said we'd find him, didn't I, Tiggs?"

And Tiggs was there too, with his ears round his neck, feeding Jack chocolate. "Where you been hanging? You got your phone off? What's happenin'? What's going *down*?" he said in a voice that was not exactly his.

"Listen, listen…" said Chris. Bully unconsciously lowered his head a little. "You got to get out of town, man."

"Yeah, I know. I seen Janks and—" He paused, left out what Janks had done to the man in the park.

"Did yer? What you been up to, Bully?"

"Nothin'."

"Must be something. If he's after you."

"What? Who?"

"You, man… *You*." said Chris. He got his phone out and showed Bully a text.

Stray gone missing $$$$ reward. JANKS

Bully couldn't work out what it meant. And then he realized *he* was the stray.

"What's *that* about?" said Chris.

"I owe him."

"OK…" said Chris. "What? Back tax?"

"Yeah, yeah. Back tax."

"How much? What you been doing? Partying it up?" Chris laughed like he didn't really think that but Bully shook his head anyway.

"Nothing," he said. He didn't need to tell Chris or Tiggs about his ticket now – he could cash it in himself. He would keep it quiet until he got to Camelot. No publicity. He'd learned that now.

"All right. Whatever. You don't want to tell, but it's all over town. That's all I'm saying. You gotta get out."

Chris nodded to Tiggs, who untied Jack's lead, and they began to walk Bully away from the shop.

"Where you going?"

"This way. Come on, we got a motor."

This was good news! Chris could just drive him there and drop him off at Camelot and he could give him something later, for petrol.

"It's down here," Chris said. Bully took the lead off Tiggs because he could walk his own dog. And they started walking back towards the house, down Swain's Lane.

"Can you drop me at Watford?"

"What? Watford? What you want to go there for?"

"Nothing."

"Nothing?" echoed Chris. "Must be *something*, Bully boy…"

"I'm meeting up."

"Oh yeah? Who with?"

He tried to think of someone, to catch up with his lie running ahead of him. "My dad. My dad lives there. In Watford."

"Oh right. We didn't know you had a dad, did we, Tiggs?" Tiggs was nodding but only to what was playing out in his head, now he had his ears on. "Oh right, Tiggs knows all about it. Anyways, we'll get you there, won't we, Tiggs? We'll get you sorted."

"Yeah?" said Bully.

"Yeah. No problem, my man."

They went past the corner of Jo's street and Bully looked down in case anyone was watching from the window. He was pleased that the blue van was gone, didn't want to see John. Bully stopped right where it had been parked.

"I just got to go and drop this off." He lifted the plastic bag up in the air.

"What?"

"I been shopping for some people." He pointed across the gardens.

"Whatever, we haven't got time for that. You know if Janks gets hold of you he's going to set the dogs on you? You know that's what he does to late payers? Come on! We're parked up."

Bully stopped again. "I'll just drop it off."

"*Drop it!* Dump it, man, come on! We gotta get movin'."

"Hold on…"

Chris gave him the dead look to show he was getting impatient. "We ain't got *time*."

Bully ignored him, eyed up the distance to the wall three houses away and started to loop the plastic bag round and round in a circle, to wrist-rocket it into their garden.

"Come on…"

Round and round the plastic bag went, faster and faster,

but Bully didn't want to let go.

"Bully! Hurry the f—"

The bag flew up, cleared the first fence, carried on rising over the second, but he didn't wait to see it fall. When he heard the *thump* he remembered that Jack's dog food was still in the bag. He would come back with the change later, with lots more money. Lots more bread too. As brown as he could get it.

The car was a big old Granada estate, with loose leather seats cracked and messed up by the sun, and they reminded Bully of the old Davey in the hospital. Bully sat in the back, cleared a space in the rubbish, and kicked green and brown bottles underneath the seat. Tiggs didn't sit shotgun with Chris but sat next to him and Jack. He kept his headphones on.

"We'll get there before tonight, yeah?" asked Bully.

"Yeah, yeah," said Chris.

They drove down Swain's Lane, back down towards the city. Bully had never seen anywhere in London in a car before, just in a bus. And he decided he liked being in a car in London because it wasn't the same as crossing roads on your feet. He kept stretching his neck to take in the unfamiliar view of the road between the seats – still missing bits of where they were going – had to keep leaning from one side to another, with Chris throwing the car about in the corners and going *whooah*…

After a while, despite all the twists and turns, he still couldn't help noticing something about their direction. The little arrow on his compass was pointing almost exactly the wrong way.

"It's north, Chris. Watford's north. We gotta go north," he said.

Chris looked round. "What you got there? You a little boy scout? Let's have a look." Bully passed the penknife over and Chris put it where he kept his cigarettes, in the ashtray, not looking at all.

"You can tell your little compass that we've got to get on the motorway first, yeah? And the motorway is south, yeah? We're gunna pick it up at Brent Cross."

"Oh yeah?" said Bully. He'd always wanted to go to Brent Cross. And now he still just about had time.

"Can we stop off?"

"Yeah, yeah," said Chris.

He could get his photos done there. He wasn't going to tell Chris why if he asked, but he didn't seem to want to know.

A bus went past, putting out the sun. He looked up to the top deck, and suddenly wished he was up there, seeing more. He wound down the window so that Jack could poke her head out. She had never been in a car either. Not in London, not anywhere. And then Bully remembered that she must have, at least once, because of where he'd found her, under the 4x4. He didn't know how someone could leave a dog like that, dumped in a car park, all ready to be run over.

Chris turned round when he heard the outside rushing in. "Bully boy! What you doin'? Wind it up, man. Wind it up! Don't want anyone seeing you, do we? It's secret squirrel."

"What?" said Bully, hadn't heard of that.

"Sick … listen up, this a *barking* beat," said Tiggs. And Chris looked round, and Tiggs started giggling and clamped the big headphones over Bully's head. He didn't know this one, didn't like things on his ears. There were no words in it and he didn't think that much of the beat. Bully liked words; he liked rap but his favourite song was "Under the Boardwalk". He didn't know what a boardwalk was but his mum used to like it because it made her cry – why that would be a good song for her, he didn't understand.

He looked out, squinted hard and thought he saw a sign for Romford, and that sounded like Watford and made him feel better for a bit.

"Yeah, sick." He felt his heart beating along. "How long do you reckon to get there?" he said, but even though he was the one with the headphones on, neither of them seemed to hear what he was saying, so he took them off.

Slowing down for the traffic lights he caught sight of seagulls and then between the buildings, smudges of the river. He thought perhaps it was a different one to his river. He tried to get a proper look but Chris was wheel-spinning away towards the next set of lights.

Then the roads got smaller, narrower, and he could read the signs. They took a sharp turn up *Gutter Lane* and then down *Milk Street*, with Chris hitting the kerb, texting as he drove. It was like they were in some sort of game with funny names but one that he had stopped wanting to play.

"We nearly there?" He knew they weren't anywhere near

anywhere but he didn't have the heart to tell himself the truth. And he pictured his knights checking their watches, getting itchy under their armour, almost ready to wind up the drawbridge when tomorrow came to an end.

"Bloody kids," Chris said and Bully realized he meant him. It was quiet then in the car until Chris pulled up on the kerb.

Chris leaned over the back seat. "We just got to stop here, drop something off. Five minutes. And then we're off to Brent Cross. You go in with Tiggs and give him a hand. You know what he's like, eh?" He smiled, raised his eyebrows, making Bully feel like perhaps Chris had meant Tiggs was the kid and not him after all.

Bully looked in the car rubbish for what it was they were dropping off, peering over the back seat into the boot.

"What you dropping off?" he asked as he opened the car door.

"Nah, I meant we're picking somin' up. Leave Jacky with me," said Chris.

Bully hesitated. "What?" he said because no one else in London had ever called her that. And for some reason it made him feel very, very sad.

"I said leave the dog."

"I dunno…"

"It'll be five minutes. Go on. Get your arse moving."

"OK, but don't feed her no more chocolate though."

"Yeah, yeah," he said.

Bully and Tiggs got out, went towards the empty face

of an office block being built, the windows missing, and lots of noise coming out of the gaps that Bully didn't like – pile-driving – *thump, thump, thump* – and drilling.

"Tiggs! Tiggs!" Chris had wound down his car window and was waving him back.

"What!" Tiggs took off his headphones. "Wait there," he said to Bully and went back to the car.

"What did Chris want?" Bully asked when he came back.

"Nuthin'... Down here." Tiggs motioned towards a narrow brick alleyway between the buildings.

"Where's it go?" Bully shouted with his hands on his ears. Tiggs just pointed up ahead. And Bully looked up and saw the house then, a big house at the end of the alleyway with lots of chimneys at the top. And all the big square windows were boarded up with black sheet metal except for this one at the bottom.

They carried on past an old lamp-post in the alleyway, the glass in it smashed, no light there and the drilling getting louder and *thump, thump, thumpier* between the walls.

Up closer, Bully could see the window was wedged open with a stick. And he could see the alleyway didn't end here but was blocked off to stop people getting through to the front of the house.

"In you get," said Tiggs.

Bully was slow getting in, trying to keep his hands on his ears and climb with his elbows and knees and feet, and Tiggs swore and gave him a lift. He sat on the windowsill, still with his hands on his ears because the *thump, thump, thumping* was even worse inside, shaking through the whole house and into him. Tiggs gave him a nudge and followed him in. The room was empty apart from some ripped-up, soggy-looking sleeping bags. Bully could see from the fag ends around the sill that it was well used, like a doorway, a hang-out.

"It's too *loud*," said Bully and he went to go back out the window.

Tiggs grabbed Bully when he saw what he was doing. "No, wait! Wait. No, listen. Chris says you've *got* to give me a hand." Bully shook his head, his palms flat on his ears. "You don't like noises, do yer... Look, put these on. Come on... It won't be long now," Tiggs said and he clamped his headphones over Bully's head and shoved the iPod in his pocket.

The same sick sound was playing.

"Yeah," Bully said, nodding because the thumping and the drilling was deadened by the thick foam and he felt better for a little while, keeping what was outside his head from getting in. Tiggs motioned to keep them on as they walked through into the dark clattery house.

From what he could see by the glow of Tiggs's mobile, they were in a hallway and just this bit of the house was huge, as big as his old flat. There were no carpets or rugs, only black wooden boards on the floor, like in a ship. And the walls were made of wood too, and looked like hundreds and hundreds of empty old picture frames stuck together.

"Up 'ere," motioned Tiggs, waving his mobile. Bully saw

in the darkness a little circle of light, like a spotlight, coming from a tiny round window at the top of the stairs that they had not bothered to board up, too small for even a skinny boy like him to fit through. Bully went up, not liking the dark. Tiggs prodded him in the back. Bully turned round and told him to cut it out.

"Can't I wait *down here*?" he mouthed. Tiggs shook his head. He mimed out the act of trying to lift a dead weight, hunching his shoulders and putting his hands to his knees, showing him just how much he needed his help. And then he pointed to Bully's ears. "The real *sick* bit …" Tiggs shouted, so that Bully could just about hear, "it's coming up…"

Bully nodded and sniffed. He didn't care about the sick beat. He would take the headphones off as soon as they found what they were looking for and got out of this place. He wiped his nose with his hand. His cold was getting worse but something familiar was squirming up his nose, a smell that he couldn't quite put his finger on with the beat in his head messing with his senses.

He sniffed again, rubbed his nose again. Something oily and warm was in the air around him … a scent. The smell was there in his head now, desperately tugging at his memory, but he was almost too embarrassed to tell himself what it was. Like those questions at school that the teacher doesn't tell you the answer to because it's so obvious, right there in front of you.

Tiggs gave him another shove. Bully turned round, taller than him on the stairs. He gave him a look and yanked off the headphones because at that moment he didn't care about the noise outside or the real sick bit coming up... And he heard a dog begin to howl and bark. And then another, and another starting up, barking to a different beat, the one coming from his heart.

Bully turned and jumped down the flight of stairs, going past Tiggs in the air, and it felt suddenly as if the whole place was falling down, but it was him doing the falling, his bad foot giving out, him falling towards the man in the spotlight, coming up the stairs with the lizard smile and the unwrapped eyes.

This was Janks's place.

20

01 DAYS **09** HOURS **09** MINUTES

Bully was blind. He kept blinking hard, opening and closing his eyes, but just like inside the gun he still couldn't see anything and all he could hear was drilling and thumping. It stopped for a minute. Somewhere beneath them, dogs took up the slack in the silence, yapping and howling, and he remembered where he was then, and that no matter how many times he opened and closed his eyes he would still be tied up in Janks's house.

Then his mum spoke to him.

… I love you … I love you so much … I love you more than … more than anyone … more than anything else in the world… Happy Birthday, Bradley! Happy birthday, love… Lots and lots and lots of love from your mummy… Mmpur, mmpurrr, mmpurr… Mmmmmrrr…

He tried to yell and scream but something stopped the sound from getting out of his mouth and he found he was having to breath through his nose. His head thumped and he felt sick with the gag in his mouth. And then someone started trying to rip his face off. That's what it felt like, anyway, when the duct tape came away from his eyes. And then a beam of light shining into them blinded him all over again.

"It's good this," said Janks. "This card of yours. The way it talks. Your mum, is it? The dead one?"

Bully tried to stand up and began to choke himself, and saw that he was naked except for his boxers. Janks pushed him back down with the toe of his boot.

"*Whoa*, boy! Stay, stay…" And Bully slipped back down the radiator.

Janks tapped him on the head with his knuckles, to see if there was anyone in.

"So you're in the land of the livin'? You got a *thick* skull, that's all I'm sayin'. Ain't he, eh? See, look," said Janks. "They thought you was dead too."

Bully blearily peered around Janks's face, a shrunken balloon of light coming from a phone. Everything was more blurry than normal. As his eyes adjusted to the light, Bully made out the orange ears and red rag that were Tiggs and Chris wavering in the background like two anxious ghosts from his past.

Terrible thoughts dripped into his head and melted the shock for a second. They had tricked him. They had lied and cheated to get him here. They had *betrayed* him; his friends.

"Hey, no need for all that," said Janks when there was a pause in the work outside and he heard Bully swearing. He shone his phone back on Bully but not right in his eyes this time.

He squatted down closer so that there was just a few centimetres between their faces, and Bully saw the creases in his face shifting about, getting comfortable. And Janks smoothed back his little stickleback bit of hair, and it stayed stuck.

"They was worried about you. We've all been worried – ain't we?" Chris and Tiggs nodded their heads. "I've had everyone out lookin' for you. That's how worried I been. Now I hear you're looking for someone to do you a favour? Eh?"

"He's taped up, Janks. He can't speak, can 'e?" said Chris in a nervy rush.

Janks stood up. The light strayed and Bully saw he was in a long, low room not much higher than him, the ceiling cracked and fuzzy and grey, like rain might come out of it.

"What? Do you think I'm *stupid*?" he shouted all of a sudden, boom-box loud.

"I was just sayin'," Chris said, in case it was a trick question and he got it wrong. And Janks yanked Chris's rag off his head and wiped his face with it. Then he slowly ground it into Chris's face, round and round like it was very dirty, until Chris pleaded with him to stop.

"And what about you, big ears? You got something to say?" Before Tiggs could answer Janks ripped his headphones off his head and smashed them against the wall until the big orange ears were hanging off.

"Right… We got that sorted. Now let's get back to business."

He knelt back down, put his finger to his lips (though the drilling was louder than any noise Bully could make) and ripped the tape off in one sharp move. And Bully coughed and coughed, felt the short relief of breathing in and out through his mouth.

"As I was sayin'. I hear you got something you want cashin' in? Am I right?"

Bully shook his head.

"No?" Janks smiled to himself as if reminded of some moment in his past similar to this one. "Well, I must have got that wrong then. You must have told me wrong, Chris." Chris stood very still, didn't want to say *anything* this time. "Right, well, we all got places to go." Janks stood up again as if waiting for him to do the same. "Well, go on then! I haven't got time to waste on little kids like you. Sling your hook!"

"I can't, Janks... I'm tied up," he said at last.

"Is that right?" Janks looked at him, all surprised, like this was news to him. But Bully couldn't help playing along, hoping there was a chance, even if it was just one in a million, that Janks really was going to let him go.

And Janks was making a meal of it now, enjoying himself, taking his time, spreading a look of fake concern slowly across his face. "Who put you on a lead then, Bully boy? Was it one of you two?" And Chris *had* to nod his head then, and Tiggs shook his as if that way they were covering themselves, right or wrong.

Janks's eyes narrowed then popped.

"Well … what you two waiting for? Untie him then, untie him. I haven't got all day."

Chris and Tiggs bent down hesitantly either side of Bully where his hands and neck were knotted against the radiator.

"I can't do the knots, Janksy," whined Chris.

"Waste of space, ain't they?" Janks casually said to Bully. "I don't know why I keep 'em."

"He keeps pulling," said Tiggs.

"Come on then, while we're waiting," said Janks to Bully. "Let's have a look at it."

"What?" said Bully, knowing what.

"This big-money ticket, eh? Let's have a look-see. Where is it? Where do you leave it? What you done with it? Where you stashed it, because for the life of me, I can't find it here, in this lot…" He motioned to the lumpy outline of Bully's old coat and the small pile of his clean new clothes.

"I didn't win nothing. There was nothin' on it," he pleaded.

"Is that right?" Bully nodded, turned his head, hoping desperately that Chris had got maybe one of the knots undone and was really still his friend.

"Ha… So there *is* a ticket? Caught you out, didn't I? Because a little birdy told me you were going to Watford to cash it in. So if you won nothing, why would you be going to Camelot, eh? So tell me, Bully boy."

"I was going to see my—" Janks slapped his face very quickly and very hard, like he'd been trying to swat this fly bothering him all day and had finally got it dead, bang on the palm of his hand.

"To see your *dad*? I don't think so. Why'd you nick the passport? Oh yeah, we found that. And your little *key*. Chris has been telling me all about your nice little family. I know all about you, Bully – I know *everything*. So, I don't want to hear any more stories coming out of *that*."

He pointed to Bully's mouth, and then picked up Bully's card. He flapped it open.

I love you … I love you so much…

And then Janks began to tear the card very slowly into pieces so that Bully's mum had nearly got to loving him more than anything else in the whole world when her voice finally died.

Janks tutted. "Now, see? Look what you made me do. You got me all tempered up. So let's start back with an easy one. All you've got to tell me is just two little things; two things – where's the ticket and where d'you buy it? Two things. One, two, easy as pie for a clever, sneaky little thing like you."

"Dowley Road Spar," Bully said, his fear grassing him up. He could tell Janks one thing though, that didn't matter – just one thing without the other didn't matter much, like a credit card without a pin.

"Where's that then?"

He told him, stuttered a bit as he described the road, the shop, Old Mac who sold it to him almost six months ago when he was nearly twelve.

"That's good. That's a while ago. No one's going to remember that ticket, are they? They got security tapes in there? Well, even if they have," he said, answering his own question, "they're not going to be keeping them for getting on for six months, are they? Good, that is good. Good boy. You done well. Right, now just one more thing – where is it?"

"It wadn't worth nothin' so I binned it. I just binned it! I can't remember what I done with it."

"Well, it's lucky, innit," said Janks and knuckled Bully's forehead again, but grinding them in like kids did at school, "that I'm 'ere. Because one thing I'm *really* good at is making people remember things. You would be *amazed* at all the remembering that goes on in this place."

He looked around him and sighed, pointed his phone to the back of the room, at the ceiling. "See that?"

Bully strained his eyes and twisted his neck as far as the muscles would take his head in that direction. He made out a long wooden beam, like the benches at school, running the length of the room. And hanging from it by its jaws was a dead dog, sweat and drool pooling underneath.

He stifled half a scream, but it was the wrong colouring to be Jack and he squinted harder and saw it was heavier set too, a pit bull. And it wasn't dead, either. He could hear it wheezing softly through its teeth.

Bully blew what compassion he had left, felt sorry for this dog, thick white scars clotted like cream around its ears from fights it must have won.

"See, that's *Scoff*. You know Scoff? You know why he's up

211

there?" Janks said, turning back to Bully, patting his head almost affectionately now. Bully shook his head.

"Well, he let me down in the park the other night – which reminds me, where was you hiding out? On the roof? Up that tree?"

"In one of the guns." He hoped that didn't make Janks angry but he seemed pleased, like it was a good story.

"No! What, one of them big ones in the front? You got all that way up there, did you? Right under my nose?" He gave him a big broad smile. "I had a feeling you was. Scoff didn't find you, did he? He fell off that gun. He let me down. He didn't do as he was told. So I'm reminding him, like I'm gunna be reminding you in a minute. Do you know what I'm reminding him of? You all know, don't ya?" he said, looking round, searching each face until he got a nod or a yes out of it.

"Course you do. Because animals is the same as *you*, they all need reminding. Now when I first started out with dogs, I used to have a favourite. *Arny* he was called. And he was always up for getting fed ahead of the rest of the pack, never letting the others near me if he could help it. But one day I wakes up after a night of it and what do I find? No more Arny ... just bits and pieces ... all over the place. He'd got old and slow and they'd torn him apart. And you know why they did that?" he said, just to Bully now, patiently waiting for him to shake his head.

"Because Arny was my top dog. And given half a chance, *everyone* wants to be top dog."

And then all traces of a smile left his face. "Right, you two…"

Tiggs and Chris hesitated. Janks's gaze drifted down to Bully's bare feet. "Well, sit on 'im then! I ain't got all day!" And Bully writhed and twisted, nearly shaking both of them off when he saw Janks pull the skewer from his boot.

"See this … you know what this is, don't you? It's for putting through meat. See." He slid it between the gap in his thumb and forefinger and Bully was mesmerized, couldn't look away. "Right, hold his foot… Last chance," said Janks. "Where is *my* ticket? I don't want to hear any more of your little stories."

"I never won … nothing," Bully said as slowly as he could, making it last. He felt the skewer tickle the sole of his left foot.

"Arrgh!" said Chris, jumping up. "He's wet himself!"

"Never mind that," said Janks. He lifted the skewer up slow and high above his head and then drove it down quick. Bully screamed but felt nothing, and when he looked, there was the skewer, sticking out of the floorboards between his ankles.

Janks stood up.

"What?" said Chris, forgetting himself. "You not getting it out of 'im?"

Janks's voice took on a mocking hurt tone. "Oh, you want to try, do you? What you saying? *You* know how to get things out of people, do you?"

"No, no… I'm just sayin', Janks, aren't you gunna torture 'im, though?"

"*Torture* 'im! Torture a little boy! What *am* I? An animal?"

Janks bent down and pulled out the skewer and it squeaked and squealed as it came out of the wood like a puppy waking up.

He slid it back down the leg of his boot. "Say I *do* torture 'im. Say I do. Just say I *do*. Say that. And then what? He starts yelling and screaming, getting blood all over the place and telling me the first thing that comes into his head; that it's here or there. And then it's somewhere *else* … and gets us racing all over town until the time's run out on this ticket of his. What's the good in that, eh?"

Chris and Tiggs nodded. There was no good in that.

"So, no. No, I'm not gunna torture 'im, Chris. I'm gunna torture that *dog* of his and kill two birds with one stone and make some money out of this either way."

Outside the drilling on the building site stopped for the day and all was quiet. And then, as if they'd heard what their master said, on the floor below, the dogs started howling again.

21

Hours later, Janks barrelled Bully up in the boot of Chris's car without telling him where they were going. When the car stopped and he heard the dogs starting up, that was the worst, waiting to see what would happen when the boot opened again.

A man with a squashed-up face he'd never seen before was looking him over, like, what was a half-naked boy doing here, and wanting nothing to do with him. Janks pulled him out, hauled him up and cut the tape around his feet but not his hands. Another man was pointing him out, staring at him, shaking his head and then turning away.

Bully felt like a whelp, like a newborn puppy, when he stood up, his bare feet tender on the concrete. He looked around. His eyes were puffy from crying and he had to open them on purpose to see anything. He felt he was inside somewhere big, somewhere empty; an old factory or a warehouse, a wet, dirty smell to the place creeping in past his cold.

"Here," said Janks. And he led him over to a proper circle of lights, made up of cars, some of them with their boots

215

open, dogs – illegals by the looks of them; nasty mixed up messes – sat there panting and snarling. One car had its boot closed, thumping and barking coming from inside … until it went quiet. He heard a man saying how you *had* to bait a dog, put it up against something before its first proper fight, just to give it a taste. And Bully could see now that in the middle of all the cars was a pit in the concrete floor, seven, eight metres long, two or three wide, with steps at one end.

Janks grabbed him by the hair, turned him round.

"So you want to play games, do you? With *me*, do you?" said Janks. "You want to—"

He paused as the man with the squashed-up face tapped him on the shoulder. "It's not right, *this*. It's not right having a lad here."

Janks hit him just beneath his chin so that he clutched his throat as if an invisible man was strangling him. Then Janks turned back to Bully.

"So let's play."

Bully knew what the bait was before Janks signalled Chris to throw Bully's old green coat into the pit. It made a thud when it hit the floor, something wrapped inside.

"Last chance – where's this ticket?" said Janks. "*Where* is it?" Bully continued to stare at his coat twitching on the concrete. "She's all taped up in there, dudn't stand a chance. She's dog meat. Come on… No? All right then. You've had your chance."

"Get on with it!" said a voice among the men. Janks motioned to one of them with a nod of his head and at the other end of the pit a black shadow approached the steps, its coat getting darker and darker in the bright light.

Bully couldn't help staring at it like it wasn't real. The way its skin folded up around its face and dripped down under its chin. The way its big black eyes drew you in, like a kid had crayoned them as good as he could. He'd seen one before, just in a picture; something just like it. One of half a dozen lessons he could pick out from his days at school. In the book, the Romans were attacking the English in their little straw huts with these big, big bulldogs. And he'd asked the teacher what kind it was and when she didn't know, he'd looked it up. It was a bandog, an old mix, not strictly a breed at all, but with a mastiff's size and weight and a bulldog's speed, born to fight anything. And this wasn't a picture in a book, this was *real*.

The bandog was pawing the concrete floor, moving forward towards the bundle, smelling the dog but then retreating while it figured out *where* the dog was. And Bully realized it was its first fight.

"You wouldn't think they'd pay good money for this, would you? *I* wouldn't waste my dog on this. It's not even a fight," said Janks.

The bandog snapped at Bully's coat then, and shook it and shook it, thinking it was dog *skin*, and a cheer went up from the crowd.

And now the dog had worked out that there wasn't any meat between its teeth and it spat it out because *that* was what it was after, squirming on the floor, trying to get to her feet.

"This is it," said Janks. "*Last*, last chance…"

Bully jumped into the pit. His knees buckled under his jaw, catching his tongue, and blood filled his mouth and he spat it out, spots on the floor.

A *huge* cheer from some in the crowd drowned out a smattering of concern.

"Get him out!" yelled someone, but in that tired, irritated voice that people use in a crowd when a dog or even a child is about to spoil a game. And some men left, and a few of the lights got smaller and smaller as cars reversed away. Didn't want to see that. Not a fair fight. But the rest, they stayed. They wanted to watch this.

The bandog had its back to the steps now, struggling to decide who was the enemy; this skinny black-and-blue thing with wrists full of rubber bands or the other dog. It didn't know what it was up against because even though its ancestors might have bated bears and lions and even Christians, this one had never fought a boy before. And Bully had to take advantage of this little bit of time, this little bit of confusion, before he became just another funny-looking dog.

He scraped his hands up and down in a sawing motion on the rough concrete wall, making them bleed but tearing the tape. And then he unwound what was around Jack's muzzle and legs, wrapping the tape around his fists just to get it off quick. Straight away Jack scrambled to her feet, barking, *up for it*, back end bristling, nosing past him, anxious *to take point*. The two dogs started heads up, haunches down, looking for weakness, showing their defences, snapping at the air.

But Bully was making things easy for the bandog, standing there behind Jack – the pair of them just one target. He needed to *outflank* it – that's what Bully had to do. Work his way round the side of his enemy to attack from behind. *But what with?* He didn't have his knife. They'd taken that, taken everything. He could use his coat maybe. The pockets were all ripped open, just like the dead man in the park, but even so, if he could get round the bandog and use his coat to strangle it or something…

So Bully shrank against the pit wall, scraping his back against the concrete as he began to edge past the bandog. He was nearly past the head and neck, at the limit of the dog's peripheral vision, when its pointed ears twitched and it went for him. It turned incredibly quick; the thin ribbon of white on its belly flashing towards him, the jaws opening, and the last thing Bully saw was his own arm going to protect his face.

He waited to feel the pain, could still see his arm and when he pulled it away from his eyes, there was the bandog squirming on the floor, Jack hanging from its belly.

Bully ran at it – his chance – went to kick at its ribs with his bare feet but he slipped and fell.

He heard men begin to cough and clear their throats over and over again. They were laughing … they were laughing at him, that's what they were doing, and he began to swear and shout back every name he could think of, as if the words might cut each bobbly face to pieces.

Clink... He looked down. He was standing on his coat. The metallic sound sent him looking for his penknife but all he found in the inside pocket was the squashed-up tin can he'd saved all that time five days ago. Without thinking he put his coat back on, as if it were a suit of armour. And at least he was behind the bandog now. And that was something. He watched the bandog shake Jack off, leaving her with a mouthful of fur and skin, and then, getting its confidence, coming straight back to catch her leg. Above the din, he heard the bone snap and Jack squeal like words might come out.

Bully reached for the can and he worked it open and slipped his right fist into it. When some of the men saw what he was doing, they started up heckling and whining, as Bully ran up to the bandog to stave in its ribs. The dog shuddered with the first punch, twisted away, taking his teeth out of Jack to show them to Bully.

Bully tried to land another one but he wasn't quick enough. He was tired now, his breathing sending his whole chest up and down, and the dog came back at him, much too *fast* – so fast it didn't see Bully's tin fist swinging under its chin.

It shivered and went down wheezing, and Bully thought they'd won. But then, as he watched it struggle to its feet, he saw that a dog wasn't like a boy, it didn't know it was beaten until it *couldn't* go on. And before he could think what to do next, it came straight back at him.

Pap! Pap! he heard as the dog brought him down, and when he scrambled out from underneath it, he saw its guts glistening like uncooked sausages, a twitching shiny hole the size of his fist there pulsing away.

He got to his feet, leaned against the wall. The crowd was silent, motionless, cut out of the light as if they were cardboard figures, only one man moving, waving a gun around, giving directions that he was not to be messed with. Two men were standing either side of him, checking their sightlines, looking out for the alpha dog.

"Your bitch?" He was looking down at Jack.

Bully nodded.

"And *you* Goldy, yeah?"

Bully looked at him, didn't understand.

"You the golden boy, *yeah*? You got the *ticket*?"

"Yeah, yeah," he said numbly.

"You tellin' me the truth, Goldy?"

"There ain't no ticket!" Janks said, piping up. "Why d'you think he's 'ere!"

Woah… went the crowd because the man was levelling

the gun at Janks's head now, no more waving it about.

"Shh," he said.

Bully got himself to the corner of the pit to look at Jack. She was whimpering, licking her wounds. Her back leg was crushed and mangled and there was a long pink tear in her cheek, like she was showing her teeth and grinning. Bully stroked the top of her head because her fur was torn and grazed across her back and ribs.

"Yeah. I won it… I got it," he said, his voice squeaking in the empty space, making him sound like a little kid.

"So where's the *tic-ket*?" said the man with the gun, tapping the word out with the end of the barrel.

Bully looked back to the man. "I ain't got it." And the barrel shifted towards his chest and he pushed Jack back into what bit of shadow there was behind him. "*She's* got it. It's in her *collar*."

"He's havin' you on!" yelled Janks. "There ain't no ticket! Shoot 'im! Shoot the *little*—" And the gunman flipped his pistol in the air, caught it and clubbed Janks with the stock, flooring him.

"Now, Goldy… You see this puppy?" he said, still talking with his gun. "Now you tell me lies and I'm putting a hole in your dog. And then you keep on telling me more lies, I put one in you? Understand?"

"It's in her collar. I hid it. I hid it in her collar." Bully looked to Janks and watched his life, the one he *could* have had – the one with millions in it – blaze up and die in front of his eyes. Whatever happened to Bully now, he was glad.

"*Arigh'*, now we getting somewhere… Out the way, boy," said the man with the gun and took aim at Jack. When Bully didn't move he adjusted his aim a little and closed one eye, like he didn't *really* want to hit a boy but it wouldn't be the worst thing in the world. And then he lowered his pistol.

"Don't wanna put a hole in this ticket, do we, Goldy."

He motioned to one of his men to go down into the pit, both of them shaking their heads and saying no way, no way were they going anywhere near *that*.

"Fetch," he said to Bully. "Give me the collar. Throw it up, easy."

Bully felt for the buckle, tried to get his fingers to grip the leather but they were greasy with blood and he couldn't work the strap.

"Don't make me come down there, boy."

"I'm tryin', I'm tryin'…" Bully looked up to plead for more time. The man with the gun was watching him very carefully now and the two men with him, as if he was digging up buried treasure in this pit. What they weren't seeing, though, was Janks on his knees, looking at the man with the gun and slowly, slowly feeling inside his boot and slowly, slowly, slowly pulling something silvery out of it.

00 **21** **37**
DAYS HOURS MINUTES

Bully was already running when he heard the first shot. Like a sprinter with a flying start, he wasn't looking at the gun.

He'd started running the second Janks raised his arm like Superman to drive the skillet through the gunman's throat.

Men were screaming, shouting, but he was out of the pit, out of the car lights and into the darkness, his bare feet padding across the concrete floor, Jack skittering along behind him on three legs.

He was fifty or sixty metres away when he heard Janks's voice strung out with rage: "Get the dog! Get the dog!" And then a few seconds later the quick chatter of a car starting up, ragging the engine, spinning smoke and rubber into the air.

The car lights quickly moved round, stretching into the darkness, turning the concrete floor from grey to white, lighting up the bare brick walls, and *him*. But now he could see his way out and he adjusted his direction to aim for the sliding doors ten metres off. It would take a grown man, perhaps two, to pull them back but still he tried. He shook them and they rattled, but that was all.

Bully turned round then to see a tonne of white-eyed metal scorching his shadow away.

But what could he do? Dive left or right? Like a goalkeeper with a penalty, he'd already made his decision. He cradled Jack up in his arms and bent down until the headlights became just one beam of light … and then he jumped *up*.

The bonnet of the car tugged his feet from under him, and he hit the windscreen, bouncing off it just before the estate ploughed through the doors. The sound it made was like an animal squealing, trying to get out, the metal against metal. And when it stopped he heard Janks still inside the car, kicking at the chewed-up door. Bully crawled away underneath the car's bumper, feeling for where the metal sliding door had been peeled back by the crash.

"Jacky, Jacky," he whispered, felt his dog brush against his face, showing him the way. Bully squirmed after her, his coat catching on the jagged metal, and he twisted, ripping through it and skinning his shoulder.

Pap! he heard, close to his head. And then he was through.

00 21 32
DAYS HOURS MINUTES

He was limping faster, the adrenaline numbing his feet, getting into a kind of hop and a skip. He thought maybe he could even *sprint*, if he had to. And he did. It was like he had scratchy cushions on his feet, couldn't feel much now, only his breath carrying him along.

"Come on, mate! Come on!" he said. Every time Bully looked back, Jack put in an extra stride, like she was trying to catch up with herself. And Bully caught a look of how bad her back leg was in the streetlights, a twisted-up mess of skin and bone that looked as if it had been stuck on wrong.

And the pair of them went down one street after another just to get away, Bully putting no thought to it until he saw the lights, patches of brightness he recognized; he was back on his side of the river, further downstream.

A car sped past. He waved his arms but it didn't slow down, just weaved round him. He couldn't chance waiting any longer for help, and he pushed on down towards the river.

00 **21** **28**
DAYS HOURS MINUTES

When he saw the couple arm in arm, he started running towards them, windmilling his arms like he was messing about. "Heeelp usss … heeelp usss," he said, his voice coming out sloppy like he was drunk, because he'd bitten his tongue. They looked at him, and they saw the dog, and they made what they thought was the right decision at this time between day and night and scurried away. He *tried* to run after them but every step was taking a longer breath and soon he knew there would be nothing left in him, and he went down on his knees and began to cry. He didn't want his millions. All he wanted was his mum back, and to be a little boy again, when it was just him and his mum in their old flat with two bedrooms and no Phil and no cat. If he could go back now to that time, the only thing he'd take with him would be Jack. And he looked at his dog, at what he still had. And he saw that it wouldn't be for much longer because it wasn't just her leg that was broke and torn…

00 **21** **20**
DAYS HOURS MINUTES

… Jack was bleeding out, blood from deep inside her organs running from red to black. He had to stop it. He was on the pavement but in the *field*. Jack was a casualty of Bully's own little war and he had to put pressure on that wound. He squeezed his hands around the top of her leg. It felt like a sodden dishcloth, and she yelped and snapped.

He needed a tourniquet. He started trying to tear at his coat but it was too thick and then he saw something better – the red elastic bands still on his wrists. He pulled them off and doubled them up to stretch them over Jack's leg but nearly all of them snapped and pinged because they were either too thin or the elastic was too old and rotten. He saw then the palms of his hands were *grey* not white…

When he started to wrap the duct tape around the top of Jack's thigh bone she turned on him. He flinched and screamed as her teeth broke the skin of his arm and cut into the muscle. The pain was *excruciating* and he wanted to hit her but he didn't let go until the tape covered the hole in her leg.

He wiped the blood off his forearm where Jack had bitten him. It felt worse than it looked. At least Jack wasn't whining any more; she was up on her three good paws and *growling*. But not at him. It was the sort of noise she made when a Fed or a fight was coming round the corner, telling him she knew more than Bully about the future, about what was going to happen next. It was time to *go*. Bully pulled himself up, and the pair of them hopped and stumbled a few steps closer to the river.

Then he saw the skinny bridge. And across the skinny bridge, he saw the big, big blurry ice-cream cone, just wasted and thrown away. Sanctuary.

He made it up the ramp, like running the wrong way up the escalators, and then: *Pap! Pap!* He turned round and there was Janks taking pot shots from the riverbank – a bullet ricocheting off the steel safety rail, one last zombie fleeing from the bridge. Bully looked across at the big, big church, his body greedily soaking up the last few sups of adrenaline. He started to run and was nearly halfway across, and the church was just beginning to sharpen up in his sights when he heard a *yelp*.

He looked back and Janks's pit bull had Jack on the bridge, its jaws clamped on her throat. Bully stopped but hesitated to go back, hopping from one foot to the other like a little boy who needed a wee while he watched the pit bull crush Jack's windpipe, taking her air away. His dog would be dead in a quick minute because there was nothing in this field he could do for Jack now. Not with just his bare hands. He looked at them and they were black with blood and useless to him.

00 **21** **13**
DAYS HOURS MINUTES

Crack!

Janks was there on the bridge, limping badly, dragging his leg along.

Bully looked down at the dark water, thick with ripples. It was too late for him, too late for his dog *perhaps*, because there was one last thing he could try. So he went back, back to her, and he got down on his knees, got his arms under both animals, still locked together, straightened up and, borrowing something from himself, he heaved this strange melded creature into the oily water.

Crack!

00 **21** **11**
DAYS HOURS MINUTES

His shoulder took what felt like a hammer blow and he was rolling, spinning over the parapet, falling through the steel cables of the bridge.

It was like one of those freefall rides – leaving his stomach behind, then the rest of him catching up, then *bam*! He hit a shopping trolley, a bike, a scaffolding pole, *something*, he thought, but it was just the water.

Under he went, sinking down, down into the darkness, his feet piercing the soft, cold muck and filth of the river bottom. He waved his arms about and kicked himself free but his lungs were boiling and he couldn't hold the little half breath he had any longer and he stayed where he was, weight and air balancing him deep under the water.

He breathed in … and he began to sink again … a freezing pain spread quickly through his chest, that feeling of swallowing a slush puppy in a rush. Then a *slow* warmth came into his body, like that feeling he had when he was half awake but still tired. He wanted so much to close his eyes, to go back to sleep, didn't mind how dark it was down here, under the water.

But something was tugging at him, biting into his bad shoulder, waking up the last little bit of pain in him, not taking no for an answer; like his mum used to get on at him for school, shaking him, dragging him out of bed, telling him to get, to get up... And slowly, slowly ... up, up, up he went.

00 **20** **51**
DAYS HOURS MINUTES

He broke back through the surface and he tried to breathe but the water had to come out first, back into the river. Coughing and choking, he clung to Jack's collar as they swept slowly downstream towards the dark towers of the bridge that opened in the middle and existed at the very edge of his imagined world. He thought perhaps he should let go before they got to the emptiness of the sea. But he hung on, drifting in and out of his surroundings.

The next thing he felt was his feet catching the bottom of the river. He turned his head and saw the black bank curving out towards him, the current at low tide kicking him across the stones like a tin can. He let go of Jack to grip at the shore. He dug his good elbow into the mud, clawing his way up like a wonky crab until he was almost out of the water. But when he looked back for his dog, Jack was gone. And in his hand was just a dirty golden dog tag.

* * *

Bam! Bam!

The delivery driver threw the bundles of newspapers at the back door of the shop. The lights were still out, the door was still locked but another couple of bundles would wake Norman up.

Bam! Bam! All the papers, all the news: crashes, deaths, births, murders, wars. All of it already out of date … except for this one little item on the front page about an unclaimed lottery ticket, running out at the end of *this* day, around the same time as someone's luck by the looks of it. After all, it had been nearly six months since the draw. And what was another day? *He* would have spent it by now, thought the driver. If it had been his ticket, he would have cashed it in the *same day* and bought a place in the countryside, somewhere nice and not too grand, near a river with swans and ducks and fish … to fish… He had not been fishing in a long while. He shut the back of the van and threw the last bundle… *Bam!* A light went on upstairs in the newsagent's. *Hhmmf,* he sniffed. Norman was up. Now he wasn't the only one awake at half past three in the morning.

The driver picked the bundle of yesterday's unsold papers off the step and when he came back to the van there was a dog in the headlights. He'd left the engine running and hadn't heard it creeping up on him. He didn't know much about dogs nowadays but it looked like one of those new sort of *devil* dogs, the sort that *went for you* if you weren't too careful. He threw the scrappy bundle of papers onto the front seat and jumped back in the van. He revved the engine to frighten it off but it stayed where it was, right in front of the vehicle. Up high, cushioned in the driver's seat, he could see in the headlights that this dog was in a bad way, jittering about on three legs, twisting round like it was making a bad job of chasing its tail.

A wire-haired Labrador flashed up in his memory: the last dog he'd had as a kid. There was no room in the city now. Too much mess to clean up. Too much of a tie at his age. Even so, sometimes, some days, he missed having a dog – something to come home to at the end of his morning round, something that missed him.

Slowly, he slid the door back, got out of the van and went over to see what was wrong with it. It didn't bark or show its teeth, and he got very close and bent down and then it came to him, hopping over on three legs, the back one hanging off like a chicken wing.

It was bleeding bad. It would be a right mess to clean up and it would probably be dead before he'd finished his round and had a chance to take it to the vet's. Still, he found himself just scooping the dog up – getting blood all over his fleece – and putting it in the front seat, where it settled down on the pile of old news.

He caught sight of the blood-streaked grey tape wrapped around the dog's back leg. He was angry then. Kids! It was always kids! He moved to pull it off but thought better of it. Let the vet do it, if it came to that…

He drove on to the next shop, towards the river. When he looked at the road, he thought it was starting to rain; every few yards there were little dark spots on the tarmac, but nothing on his windscreen, and then he realized this was the way the dog had come, from the river. And when he got down to the embankment, he saw blue lights downstream, blinking away. That was his direction, towards the trouble and the blue lights. He began to turn left but then put the vehicle into a wide arc, changing his mind when he saw the spots of blood weaving off to the right, because he just had to *know* where this mixed-up-looking dog had come from.

00 20 09
DAYS HOURS MINUTES

The trail stopped here. He parked up with his lights shining onto the foreshore. He turned the engine off this time and got out and peered at the dim water's edge. And in the light of the new day, he thought what he saw dragging itself out of the mud was some leftover creature from out of the river's past. Some *thing* that had done this to the dog. But then he saw that it was just a boy wrapped up in a grown man's coat, lying twisted on one elbow, head down, sucking air an inch from the water.

The driver waded into the mud, shouting and telling the boy he was *safe*, that he was *OK* now, like you did when someone wasn't either one of those things. When he got to the boy, like the dog, he picked him up and took him back to the van, but this time he laid him out on the pavement and covered him with clean, fresh papers.

"Jacky's got the ticket," croaked the boy. The driver heard the dog in the van moving around, pawing at the door.

"Jacky? Who's Jacky? Don't you worry," he said because he was *very* worried. He got his phone out, never bothered turning it on this first part of the day.

"Who's Jacky?" the driver asked the boy again, but the boy just looked up at the lightening sky.

"Come on, boy … stay awake." He had a feeling you were supposed to do that, to stay awake to stop that bigger sleep grabbing hold of you in the silence.

"Who's Jacky? What ticket?" he said in desperation, asking him any old question, trying to keep him *with it*.

"Come on, wake up. Where's this ticket? What you got there? Is this *it*? He saw something trying to shine in the grip of the boy's hand. "Is this the ticket? Is it Jacky's ticket? Come on, boy… Try and stay awake…"

He took it out of the boy's hand. It looked like a doubloon, a gold coin the boy had scraped off the bottom of the river, but when he wiped it clean it was just a cheap brass dog tag. The sort you could buy for just a few pounds. *Jacky* it said in the metal. But it took him the length of the phone call to the emergency services to comprehend that this was the boy's dog sitting on top of the papers in his delivery van. That this *was* Jacky.

And as the flashing lights from downstream drew closer,

he began to wonder, in that strange shock that panic brings, if the dog in his van *did* have the ticket, where it might be and what sort of ticket was worth dying for.

23

00 **00** **00**
DAYS HOURS MINUTES

Bully was floating in some sort of boat, not moving though, anchored where he was to the seabed. He could hear birds, *beep, beep, beeping.* A man in a proper shirt and trousers was wading towards him, trying to catch his eye with a rubber smile.

"How are you feeling, Bradley?" the man said.

Bully looked around – saw a couple of other boats like his with bodies in them, but he couldn't see the birds that were *beep, beep, beeping* at all.

He tried to sit up then but he was too heavy, his whole body weighed down by invisible anchor chains. Even his voice couldn't escape. He tried to talk but it came out a whisper and then he couldn't hear any more, and the shapes and sounds around him fizzed and melted away.

The next time he woke, Phil was there, next to his bed. He looked weird. He was smiling with his mouth open, showing his teeth, as if for a proper picture in a newspaper or a magazine.

"How you feeling, pal? What you been getting into? You're lucky it didn't nick an artery. *Just* grazed your shoulder blade, they said…"

Bully looked about for something that was missing, couldn't think what it was.

"It's all right, don't worry. It's *safe*. I got it covered. Why didn't you tell me we'd won it? If it hadn't been for that driver, you'd'a lost us the bloody lot! What?" he said because Bully was trying to talk.

It really hurt, like the worst sore throat, the pain shooting all the way down to his lungs. Finally he said it: "Ja…" and made a listening face, putting his head to one side.

"Who? Your mum?"

Bully shook his head.

"Ja…"

"What? The *dog*?"

Bully nodded, his shoulder throbbing now he knew that the bullet had just grazed him.

"She's not here, is she? They don't let dirty old dogs in here, do they?"

Phil paused to look round the ward in case someone might be listening. "Right, listen. You hearing me?" He leaned in, as close as he'd ever got to Bully in the last six years. "They won't want to pay out, I can tell you that now. Not unless we say it was me what bought the ticket, OK? So that's *our* story. OK?"

"*Jack—*"

"Yeah, *what*?" Phil said, getting irritated now, trying to go through his plan.

Bully made the OK sign with his fingers and blinked his eyes wide to say: Is. She. OK?

"Well, she's not here, is she? Look, all I know is that she was in a right state. The vets said she was as good as dead when they brought her in and they're not making any promises. I'm telling you that now, so you'd better be prepared for the worst." He paused to inspect something on Bully's cheek. He looked puzzled and then annoyed. "No, come on, come on, come on. Let's have none of that," he said and showed him the newspaper headlines from the past few days.

HOMELESS BOY ESCAPES BOUNTY GANG IN DRAMATIC THAMES FALL

DEVIL DOG SAVES STREET BOY IN RIVER PLUNGE!

LOTTO-GANG STREET KID WINS BIG THANKS TO MUTT!

SUSPECTED KILLER STILL ON THE RUN...

The police came in three times to speak to Bully. They praised him, and told him what a brave boy he was, like he was a little kid with cancer or something. He didn't do a lot of talking because his lungs hurt. As well as all that dirty water getting in them, he'd busted his ribs in the fight. Three of them. And you couldn't do anything about that. No knives, no injections, no tubes. They didn't even put you in a plaster cast. You just had to let them heal. And that would take time, the doctors said.

He asked the Feds about how Jack was doing but they didn't seem to know, promised they'd look into it for him. Then they told him about his own story. Half of London – the wrong half – had got to know about his numbers coming up. And they wanted to know about the dead man in the park because they said they knew Bully had been there. They'd rounded up Tiggs and Chris and some of the men at the dogfight but they were still looking for Janks. His real name was Peter Jefferson. And could he tell them anything about him or the dead man? And Bully said no, he didn't remember no dead man, didn't remember *nothing*, especially nothing about Janks.

When they'd taken most of the tubes out and he could eat without anyone helping him, a woman came on to the ward and sat down next to his bed. He clocked straight off who she was. The way she kept smiling when there was nothing to smile about, the way she looked like she'd stopped off on her way to somewhere else. She was from the social. He asked her about Jack but she didn't know anything about dogs. So he asked her when he was getting out of here. Her smile shrunk a bit and she said they were looking closely at what would be best for him now that his situation had come to light. Because his mother was dead and the whereabouts of his real father unknown, he was *at risk*. He could tell the woman thought it might make him sad to know this. He listened while she took him through his care options.

Care option 1: How did he feel about going back to the flat? (He said "dunno" to that.)

Care option 2: What did he think about living with a direct relative? If they could find one of those. (He just shrugged at that one.)

Care option 3: How about going to stay with a foster

family? (He said "no" to that: he didn't want a fake mum or dad.)

Care option 4: What were his thoughts about going to live in a *care home*? (He considered it until she told him they didn't take dogs, only kids.)

The woman went away and came back a couple of days later with her best smile. She was very pleased to tell him they had looked into all his options and that his preferred option was *definitely* now an option. He was going back to the flat.

24

He opened his eyes and heard the tail end of a scream coming out of his head.

He'd been dreaming. *In* the dream, he was asleep and the smell woke him up. On the couch, the TV turned up, dozing and then starting to cough, this chemical smell coating his throat, getting worse and worse the more he coughed, creeping further down and *fizzing*. And then above the back of the sofa, seeing that stickleback bit of hair spiking up, his old street name seeking him out... *Bully... I've come for you...* That was when he woke up from the dream to real life, back on the couch, screaming for his mum.

Cortnie was watching some kiddy crap with *it* on her lap and screaming too. And the baby was starting to cry. And Jack was barking, trying to get up on the couch. It was the dog Cortnie was screaming at because it looked weirder than ever now to her.

He yawned and rolled over and rubbed his shoulder. It itched where the bullet had gone in, and there was a small but deep hole in the skin like a tiny meteorite had torn through the atmosphere and into him a few weeks ago.

"Get *it* off," Bully said to her because this was where he slept. But what with everyone in and out, and *it* waking up all the time, and Emma nagging him off the sofa when she forgot she was supposed to be nice to him, he didn't get that much sleep here.

Emma came in from the bathroom. "What *is* going on, Bradley? You can't keep screaming like that with the baby!" She picked it up and coo cooed it and took it to the kitchen. Then she shouted back: "And don't let that dog keep jumping up! I don't want her round the baby!"

He watched Jack's face appear over the arm of the couch, her eyes frantic and wide before she fell back down and tried again. She was playing a game, trying to get his attention, but he didn't want to play. "Come 'ere," he said, waving her round to the front of the couch now that the baby was gone.

When he got out of hospital he couldn't just go and get Jack from the vet's. He was too young to be *legally responsible*. You could have a cat, a guinea pig, mice, a *rat* or any of that other four-legged crap, but in the eyes of the law you had to be sixteen to own a dog.

When he finally pestered Phil enough to get him down the pound and sign the forms, he was expecting to see Jack, not this other dog. It looked something like her but was shaved almost all over down to prickly skin and bones. It was thinner, missing five or six kilos in weight and *one* leg. At the back on the left there was just a flap of skin sewn over her stump.

"The leg was a real *mess*. I mean, even if we could have

saved it, it really wasn't worth saving," said the vet, trying to be nice about it.

Phil, not trying to be nice about it, had suggested getting rid of this dog and getting another one later on, a better one, with a proper *pedigree* and all four legs, when they moved house and got the payout. But Bully shook his head and said no. He said things inside that were a lot worse. Because Jack was still his dog. The difference was that now, he wasn't so proud of her any more, didn't want to be showing her off, out and about on the estate. He only took Jack out late at night, after the good TV had gone bad, when there was no one much about.

He hadn't wanted to go out *at all* because of all the press and the TV wanting pictures of him and Jack. Bully didn't want any publicity. So they'd had to make do with Phil and the driver who'd found the ticket and told the police about it right at the last minute, at the end of his round. There were loads of pictures of *him*. He'd already got his reward from Camelot for handing it in.

Now they'd all moved on to another story and were leaving him alone, but people still whispered and pointed him out like he was a celebrity. And he didn't like it. Perhaps when they got the money and they went to live with all the other celebrities, then he wouldn't mind being pointed at, sitting next to David Beckham maybe. But it had been nearly a month since he'd crawled out of the Thames and they were still waiting for the payout, even though the woman from Camelot had been to see them. She'd come to the flat with just a card, no money in it. She told Phil some questions *still had to be asked*. And they were going to be asked at Camelot, with him and Phil in the firing line.

Phil was already spending. And he was running up a *tab* everywhere and not just on credit cards but with people you had to pay whether you had the money or not. It wasn't like the bank; they didn't just write you nasty red reminder letters. They came round in person to see you, as a nasty reminder.

Flap, flap, flap at the letter box. That was the only interesting part of his day. Bully could tell it was the postie from the way he did it, and he gingerly got up off the couch. His shoulder and his ribs ached first thing in the afternoon when he'd been lying down for a while, and sometimes instead of opening the door, he would spend five minutes listening to the letters coming through the letter box... *Flap, flap, flap.*

He came back to the couch with a pile up to his chin and sorted through the different-sized envelopes, looking for something good. Some of them were cards from people wishing him well (and then making more wishes, asking for things for themselves). Most of them were letters written on little coloured squares of lined paper, one or two even typed on bigger sheets. Whatever sort they were, they were all called *begging letters*. And Phil threw them straight down the rubbish chute if he was in, even the ones that were addressed to Bradley.

The complaining ones just annoyed him when they

started saying how hard their lives were and asking him to buy things *he* didn't even have yet. He preferred reading the ones that asked for stuff straight out, that just tried it on for a bit of a laugh.

Dear Bradley, You won the big one! Mega congrats! I could do with an upgrade on my life too! Can you spare 500 quid? Or a grand? Cheers bro...

He never replied to any of them. Even the funny ones.

25

He had a visitor at the door.

"Someone to *see* you… A little friend of yours, hon," Emma said, kissing her lips up, showing him she wasn't so little.

"What? Who?" he said but she was already back in the kitchen.

Phil's bedroom door was closed. He was still in bed, dosed up to the eyeballs with painkillers – his back still bad – getting ready for the meeting tomorrow with Camelot.

"Hello, Bully," said Jo when he got to the door. She looked different, older in just a few weeks, grown up without being taller.

"No one calls me that round here," he said.

"Sorry, Bradley."

"Your stuff – I ain't got it. I lost it. The shoes and the money and all that."

"Oh, no, that's nothing. Mum doesn't mind. She gave it to *you* anyway. I just wondered…"

"What?" he said.

"If you got the card we sent you? I sent it to Camelot.

I didn't know your address."

"Didn't get it." He shook his head. He was starting to breathe hard. He had trouble breathing when anything *out of the ordinary* happened. He started sucking in the air for no other reason than it was panicking him seeing her here, a whole different world flapping at his door.

He slipped his trainers on, kicked Jack back inside the flat with the side of his foot and motioned Jo out onto the landing. Declan next door trundled past on his plastic motorbike and looked up at them. His mum was watching him play. She smiled extra nicely at Jo because she was a visitor. "You find him all right then, love?" She stopped smiling when she looked round. "Declan! No!" she yelled because Declan had climbed off his bike and was trying to force it down the rubbish chute.

Bully took Jo to the end of the landing and down the stairs. "How did you get here, if you didn't know where I lived, then?"

"I saw your stepdad, Phil, in the pictures."

"He's not my stepdad," said Bully.

"Sorry." She blushed like she had done in that little room at the top of her house. "Anyway, I worked out that it was somewhere round this area from the road signs in the photos. And then I *asked*." She sounded pleased with herself. "Your next-door neighbour told me in the end. I just thought I'd come and see how you were getting on, whether you needed any … thing."

They went down to the ground floor, went walking. One

or two people stared and one laughed and shouted, "Brads! Lend us a tenner!"

"How's your dog?" Jo said in the silence that followed.

"They chopped her back leg off. We didn't have to pay though," he said.

"I'm really sorry about that. But she's all right though, is she?"

He nodded, a little ashamed of himself because though he was glad he still had her, he couldn't help feeling embarrassed when people saw him out with a three-legged dog, whatever breed she was.

"So, is it all OK? Are things all right here for you living back with your – with Phil, is that his name?"

He shook his head to say things weren't OK.

"When we get the money, I'm living somewhere different."

"What do you mean?"

He shrugged. He'd forgotten that she didn't know about the deal he'd done with Phil that they were pretending it was *his* ticket. That they were splitting it 50/50 and Phil was giving him half and not the other way round.

"So when do you get it then?"

"What?"

"The prize money."

"Dunno. Soon. It's only 1.1 million though." He was disappointed when the lady from Camelot had told them that. That the jackpot that week was one of the lowest they'd ever had and *only* 1.1 million pounds.

"That's still *loads*."

He turned on her then. "Well, you must have *that*."

"No! You're joking, right? My mum and dad work full time. You *know* they do," she said, as if to remind him he had met her parents.

"Yeah, but your house. And all those books. That must be worth way more. You didn't even have to win anything. You could sell that and be more of a millionaire."

"Yeah, I suppose so, maybe, but…" She waved her hands about, struggling to explain away this comparison. "It's where we *live*."

They walked along Dowley Road, ended up walking past the Spar shop where he'd bought the ticket. He didn't want to go in in case Old Mac was on the till and suddenly remembered, like old people did, that it was *him* who bought the ticket that day. So Jo went in and got them drinks. They talked about what Jo was doing next, going to college. And that Alex was off to some place called *uni*.

"I nicked his passport," Bully said. He thought he should confess in case Alex might need it to go there.

She looked surprised and then disappointed. "Did you? Oh… OK. He's got a new one now. We just assumed it was from the break-in."

He nodded, annoyed with himself for shrinking down in her eyes. "What did they nick then?"

"Nothing much. Just some money and stuff. But they got the keys to Dad's van with all his work gear and it wasn't insured."

"I'll pay for it then. And I'll get him a new one!"

"You can't do that…"

"I can. I will."

"No, I mean it's very kind of you, Bully…" She looked embarrassed. "But I mean, it's not your money, is it? It's Phil's…"

And he remembered again that she and everyone else thought it was *Phil's* ticket and that *Phil* had bought it.

They walked along, past the little kiddie park with no little kiddies in it, on towards the station. "Are you walking me back?" she said. "The station's this way, isn't it?"

"Yeah…"

But he stopped walking because of where they were, and what was here. He looked across the road at the straggly bed of still-flowering weeds. He could just see one edge of the broken paving-stone, imprisoned in the pale green stems.

"You OK?" she said. He looked back at her like she was a photo from a long time ago. "I'll give you my number if you want… If you need someone to talk to. And Dad says you should come over and visit again. You *and* Jack."

"She dudn't go out in the day," he said automatically.

"If there's anything I can do, Bully… Bradley, I mean. Sorry. Is there, though? Anything … I can help you out with?"

"Like what?" he said to test her, to see if she really meant *anything* because there was one thing he had in mind, that he would need help with, going behind enemy lines…

"I don't know… Taking Jack out, maybe…"

"She dudn't walk."

"She *can* walk though, can't she?"

"She dudn't. She *hops*," he said dismissively.

"OK, well with school then, maybe?"

He just sniggered. Wasn't planning on doing too much *school* once Phil gave him his share of the payout.

"I don't know, whatever, you know, to help. Anything you want…" She didn't seem put out by the way he was behaving and it annoyed and impressed him at the same time.

"OK then. Yeah," he said.

She nodded expectantly, waiting for him to tell her, but instead he turned away and headed over to the patch of scrubland that looked as if it might once have been a proper flower-bed.

She followed him across the road and watched him prise up what looked like a piece of paving-stone from among the late summer weeds. He started poking around with a stick but she didn't say anything until he began to dig with his hands.

"What? Have you lost something?" she said. And he waved her over to take a closer look.

26

They got a taxi from the train station. Five minutes later the driver was pointing out a big brick office block on a roundabout; no castle, no moat, just tarmac around a bunch of bricks and glass.

"This is it," he said.

As soon as they got out, Phil said, "Remember, right? We do this by the numbers, keep it simple. Right, right, right?"

Bully nodded. Phil was like this when he got nervous, repeating things like they did in the army so you didn't forget. "Yeah, yeah, yeah," Bully said.

They went up in a lift, right to the top. The woman in reception let Cortnie press the button. A man and two women were waiting for them in the corridor outside a room with a frosted-up window so you couldn't see through it. The man telling them his name was Alan had his hand out before they even went inside. Bully watched Phil shake it and the hand was still there for him. And then he had to do it again with the two women: Carol and Diana. He recognized the lady called Diana. She'd come to the flat a few weeks ago as a *Camelot representative*. She hadn't looked like he'd imagined, mostly because she was a woman. He hadn't expected a real knight but he had expected a real man to deliver the message.

This second time, he didn't mind her. She was OK, he decided, making a fuss of Cortnie, saying how nice her new clothes were as if they were all designer. He didn't like the look of the other one, Carol. Her teeth were too white and they looked at you like eyes did, wet and shiny. And he didn't like the sound of her either, like she had chocolate stuck in her throat when she spoke.

They went inside the room and they all sat down at one end of a massive table, and that was made of see-through glass. Everything in the place was see-through except for the windows which were frosted up. He supposed it was to stop people thieving stuff. He could see the new jeans Phil had bought him through the glass, right down to his sports socks and new Reeboks.

"Would you like something to drink?" Alan asked Phil.

"A bit early for me," he said as if it was a test.

Bully said no thanks but Cortnie got a Coke out of it.

Then they got started.

They wanted to know all about the day Phil bought *his* ticket. Bully started listening but lost interest and did his best to look through one of the frosted windows. It was sunny out and he suddenly wanted to be outside, back on the riverbank, shading his eyes and doing a bit of fishing... It was just a feeling he had, him and the old Jack out there (the one with four legs), hanging out, things back to normal. Because this *wasn't* normal.

"So … we just need to ask one or two more questions." Carol was talking, had taken over, surprising Phil – Bully could tell because he was already nodding before she was anywhere near asking him anything.

"So, Phil, you've just said you purchased the ticket at the Spar shop in Dowley Road. And from the terminal read-out we can see this was at 5.26 p.m. on February the 16th." Phil was nodding still, and faster, and Bully could hear him bunching his fingers, freshening up his fists every few seconds.

Carol was looking at Bully now, with those wet, white, shiny teeth. She kept showing them at him and then Phil, backwards and forwards between them like the bandog, unsure which one of them to attack first.

"We can see from one of our terminals that the ticket was checked against a till in Waterloo station on Friday, August the 9th at 6.45 p.m. … 174 days after the draw and 176 days after it was purchased. Is that right? Did you get it checked, Bradley?"

"Yeah."

"Well, what we would like to know is how it came into your possession?"

"What d'you mean, like? What? Like how he got hold of it?" asked Phil, butting in.

"Yes. How did you get hold of it … Bradley?" said Carol. She hadn't even been looking at Phil while he'd been talking.

She was getting ready for Bully's reaction.

"He must have picked it up after I went out, by accident. He's cack-handed like that," said Phil, like it was a proper thing.

"We appreciate that but we would like to hear it from Bradley," Alan said, coming back at him, one either side now, getting ready to outflank Phil.

Bully spoke hesitantly, slowly looking through the glass table down at his feet, as if the past was down there and might give him a nip on the ankles. "I went to Smiths but the man said it wasn't a cash prize from the till and that I had to go to Camelot in Watford."

They all nodded and smiled at that as if the man in Smiths had done the right thing.

"He said I had to phone them up. But I didn't have any credit so I went instead. And that's when they started chasing me."

They all pulled very serious faces now. They had heard about that, the terrible things that had happened to him and his dog.

"Yes, that sounds awful, Bradley," said Carol.

"Absolutely awful," said Alan.

"How's she doing? Your dog," asked Diana.

He shrugged. "They chopped one of her legs off. The vet did," he added when he saw their faces freezing up, thinking it was the gangstas.

"So… OK," said Alan after they had all said how sad they were about that. "Getting back to the ticket: how did you come to have it, the winning ticket, in your possession? Because we have to ask you this, Bradley," Alan said with a very serious teacher look on his face to make sure Bully understood this was about money and so it was really *serious*. "Did you buy this lottery ticket yourself?"

"No," he said. He heard Phil puffing out a breath next to him, the old air saying that was it, they would pay out now.

"So who *did* buy the ticket?" asked Carol, leaning right forward so that her teeth were closer to him than any other bit of her.

"My *mum* did."

Bradley heard Phil's neck clicking, his head turning that quick.

"*She* went down the shops. *He* wasn't even there. He was wiv 'er. Not my mum." He didn't know where this was coming from; he didn't know what was making him say this now.

"Sorry?" Alan asked. "Are you telling us that Phil didn't buy this ticket?"

"*My mum* bought it," he said very slowly, like he had learning difficulties.

Phil blew up. He stood up, catching his knees on the edge of the glass table. "She couldn't have got down there! She'd been in bed since New Year! She was *dead* before they even called the numbers!"

"Please, Mr Greg … Phil," said Alan, trying to put the lid back on it.

"All I'm saying is, you ask her doctor!" Phil interrupted,

coming back at him. "The last few days she couldn't have got out of bed to go for a – she couldn't'a got down the shops, that's all I'm saying. She was so dosed up she didn't even know if you were there half the time!"

"*You* weren't there," said Bully. "*None* of the time."

All during that last week Phil had been "popping out". And Bully knew where. Declan's mum had been popping in, taking Cortnie off their hands. No one knew for sure when his mum died except him.

Phil sat back down and stared at him. His fists were solid under the table now, the bony tops of the knuckles showing just under the skin.

"Well, well… Maybe, maybe she did buy it and I got confused with the midweek draw. Yeah, yeah, yeah. Thinking about it now, I think I must have done. I think she *did* buy it after all," said Phil, surprising Bully, going along with his version now.

"Well, this changes things, unfortunately," said Alan, looking to his left and right at Carol and Diana. "And I think we are going to have to conclude this meeting for now and look at gathering more evidence."

No one said anything.

"Do you understand, Bradley?" said Diana, leaning forward like Carol but looking concerned, like it really wasn't anything to do with the money. "Bradley… Bradley…"

His mum had been telling him for days they were going to win.

He'd found it hard listening to her, especially that day,

the day of the draw. She kept calling him in from the lounge, shouting against the TV, talking and breathing at the same time, jumping from one thing to another, shouting *Happy Birthday!* Even though that day was nearly two weeks away.

And she'd kept trying to give him his birthday card early, telling him she'd put just a *little something* in it for now. And him refusing to open it and pretending he had to go out to buy milk and bread. And wanting to escape, to get out of the flat, but thinking he should stay. And then coming home dragging his feet but wanting to run all the way. And finding her like *that*, knowing she wasn't alive but still waiting for someone else to come along and tell him she was dead. And then opening the card and hearing her very last words; what she'd said to him.

"Bradley? Do you understand, Bradley? Are you OK?" Diana was saying to him but he just kept looking straight ahead, squinting through the windows at the frosted sunlight.

On the train back to the flat they sat at a small table. Bully sat opposite his sister and Phil. Whenever he looked up, Phil was looking straight back at him, not saying anything.

It was five stops on the train and Cortnie fell asleep and when she did, Phil kicked him under the table.

"What?" Bully said. Though he knew what.

"You left me hanging, you did. You left me right out there in no man's land, you did. We could have done this *nice* and easy but, no, you had to go it alone, didn't you? I know what your game is…"

Bully's head went down and Phil kicked his foot to bring it up again.

"You listening to me? You *think* because your mum and me weren't married, you *think* you're going to get the lot? Well, you're *not*. I had a word with *him* before we left. Even *if* they pay out – and now you've got them looking into it more, it's not a done deal, and it's not going to be for bloody *years* now – but if they *do*, in the end, then all the winnings don't just go straight to you when you're eighteen… You hadn't thought of that, had you?" He nodded sideways. "Alan says *she* gets half. She's your mum's daughter. It goes through the bloodline. She inherits it just like you. And I'm *her* dad whether I married your mum or not. So just so you know: all this still works out for me, one way or another."

And he kicked one foot and then the other, to remind Bully of that.

27

Bully left the flat in the afternoon as soon as he woke. He was already dressed. He left on his own. He hadn't planned on taking Jack because of the no-dogs-allowed situation and Phil had been OK about it.

"Nah, leave her 'ere. We're all off out later," he'd said because it was Emma's birthday and they were celebrating round her mum's place. Bully thought maybe Phil wanted Jack there for something else, for back-up maybe during the day: all the flapping of the letter box they were getting from the *Gombeen* men, as his mum used to call them, the moneylenders that Phil was throwing scraps to now he wasn't getting his money straight away.

Jo met him at the railway station and they travelled back into London, back along the Northern line, carrying the sweetie jar and the broken piece of paving-stone in the Bag for Life he'd bought from one of the supermarkets in town.

"Are you sure this is what you want to do?" Jo asked him, just like they did in the films. And just like in the films, he nodded and said he was going to do it, with or without her, though that wasn't true because he didn't think he could do it on his own, not in the day anyway. And the daytime was the proper, right time to do it. No more creeping around.

Jo paid to get in. And just like she'd said, they had to go with a tour guide, though it wasn't like any holiday Bully had ever seen. None of the zombies seemed bothered. They all acted like it was a normal day out to walk round a place full of dead people, right under their feet, taking pictures of gravestones and eating sandwiches.

The lady in charge of their tour with a sweet-sucking face was suspicious of Bully, he could tell. Perhaps it was because he wasn't taking pictures. He didn't look that different in his jeans and Reeboks. And he wasn't the youngest on the tour. It was just something about him, his breed that marked him out. Or perhaps it was the sense of purpose carved into his face; that he wasn't just here for a day out.

The lady started up straight away with her sweet-sucking about keeping to the path and no littering and explaining that she was a *friend* of the cemetery who did all this for free. Then she started talking about the dead people and the graves and Bully and Jo slipped to the back of the group.

As they followed along, Bully didn't recognize very much of the cemetery in the daytime. It looked more like a theme park without any rides or concession stands, just fake-looking statues and little paths going everywhere, park benches all over the place.

"What about over there? That looks like a nice spot?" said Jo.

Bully shook his head. It was just a spare patch of grass behind some other gravestones. And he didn't want his mum stuck in there like she was in a tin of sardines. He was looking for somewhere special and exclusive with a private view of the trees and the grass.

He'd planned to scatter his mum next to Lady Di and he'd been *very* disappointed when Jo had told him she wasn't buried here because Lady Di was still famous, even though she was dead. Not like all these old-fashioned celebrities Jo kept going on about who'd never been on TV. His mind was made up though. If it was good enough for this *Karl Marx* guy, some famous old Davey who'd spent all his days in the library a hundred years ago, Jo said, then it was good enough for his mum.

As they drifted further and further back like tired-out toddlers, and the feet and chatter of the rest of the tour got further and further away, Bully started to hear the nicer noises of the cemetery that he hadn't heard at night: birds talking to each other, the leaves making a fuss of hanging on to their branches in the little bit of wind between the trees. And then he saw the spot, the best spot for his mum, with a tree for the birds and even an angel from next door's grave looking over like Declan's mum did next door, keeping an eye out.

"There, over there!" he said.

"Right, quick then! Let's go. Let's do it!" said Jo. She was smiling and giggling but that seemed right. And they ran through the graves and off the path to the little patch of trees on a bit of a hill. Bully quickly scraped a space in the roots of the dark green ivy and the dead leaves and unscrewed the red lid right off the sweetie jar.

"Are you going to say anything?" said Jo.

"What?"

"You know … something nice. I think you're sort of supposed to."

He looked into the dust and grit and still couldn't help wondering if there was any bit of her left that he might recognize – a tooth, a bone, but there was nothing. It was just ashes, the 3% that was left of her.

"I don't know…" But Jo was still smiling and it was still right. "R.I.P., Mum," he said because that was what people said. And he went to tip the couple of kilos of her ashes out of the jar but they seemed suddenly very heavy to him. And then another hand was underneath nudging his, and the ground began to puff up with thick grey-and-white dust like a little bonfire that had finally burned out. He tapped the bottom of the plastic jar, made sure there was nothing left inside and passed it to Jo. Then he put the piece of broken paving-stone that he'd brought with him somewhere in the middle, got down on his hands and knees and pushed it deep into the earth.

"So that's your mum's name," said Jo, reading the scratches in the stone that Bully had made last night. And he nodded down, and noticed when he stood up that the bottoms of his jeans were a lighter blue than the rest of his legs. He didn't mind when he realized what it was. He brushed the ash off. It was just dust now.

"Oh, crap," said Jo, but he was still looking at the bit of paving-stone and folding up his Bag for Life and wondering what kind of birds they were that his mum would be putting up with for the rest of her life, because he couldn't remember if she really liked birds all that much or not. There weren't many birds on their estate.

"What *are* you doing with *that*?" said a sucked-up voice behind him.

28

It was Jo who ran. She was almost back on the path when she looked round and he was still there standing next to the sweet-sucker. Because for Bully, now, this wasn't a place for running away.

The *friend* of the cemetery walked them back to the reception, telling them it was thoughtless what they had done even after Jo explained.

"I'm very sorry for your loss," she said, looking at Jo not Bully. "But you can't just do as you please! There are laws in here just like *everywhere* else! It's not self-service! You have to have the proper written authority and go on the waiting list just like *anyone* else! What would happen if *everyone* did what you've just done?" she said finally. "We'd have bodies all over the place!"

"Well, there *are*," said Jo in a sarcastic voice, looking around the place.

The women tutted, sucked on her invisible sweet and said "typical". She told them to sit and wait while she got someone official to deal with them.

She came back with an old bloke, with a baggy, saggy

throat. He was a cross between a Davey and a retired zombie, wearing a black suit and a tie that looked as if he'd got it second hand off a bigger, younger man.

He introduced himself and said that he was called Mr Faraday. And he asked Bully and Jo to write down their names and addresses and a responsible adult who could pick them up because he didn't think this was really a matter for the police.

"Who have you lost?" asked the man, as if Bully just might find her again if he searched and searched hard enough. Bully knew what he meant though.

"My mum," he said and pinched himself because his eyes were making things more squirmy than usual without his glasses on. "I wanted her to end up somewhere nice. And not in a bin."

And then he told the story, a shorter story than the one he'd told the old man in the hospital in case this one didn't remember any of it either.

Towards the end there was a knock on the door and the sweet-sucker came in, still not out of sweets yet.

"I've cleaned things up as best I can," she said. She put a bag on the desk with a clunk, giving the old man an "it's in there" face, and Bully swore at her on top of his breath, not under it.

The old man nodded and waved her out whilst he kept his eye fixed on what was on the desk. He would deal with this too.

"Now, I do have a great deal of sympathy for you and

your loss," said the man, pausing to look to the door as if the sweet-sucker might come back. "But I have to say to you that the rules are for everyone... So that everyone can enjoy this beautiful place. The ashes will be left as they are but the stone cannot legally remain where it was laid. Unfortunately there are no exceptions. I can't put this back. I'm sorry," he said, smiling, his throat wobbling about as he swallowed down his apology.

But Bully's eyes flushed with hate. And that made them much smaller, letting less light in, so that the man suddenly stopped squirming in front of him and Bully saw as clear as he ever did with glasses what happened next. Because the man did a very strange thing with just one of *his* eyes, something that only old people still knew how to do nowadays: he winked at them.

29

Jo's dad picked them up from the cemetery and made promises to the man. He said it in that quick, funny voice of his. He didn't make a big fuss about Jo getting into trouble and helping Bully out; all he made a fuss about was Bully coming back for something to eat. But Bully couldn't go through that whole show again. So even though he was hungry, Jo's dad drove him straight home in his new second-hand van.

"Are you really *sure*, Bully?" said Jo on the way there. "Are you sure you don't want to come back and have something with us? You can stop the night if you like? Can't he, Dad?"

But Bully shook his head, didn't want them stopping anywhere near his flat either, and so they dropped him off right at the edge of the estate.

"Next time, eh, boy?" said Jo's dad, in that voice of his that made it sound as if the words really did mean something and he wasn't just being nice about it.

"Yeah, yeah," Bully said, making his promises quick to get out of the van, saying that he would bring Jack with him next time too.

He walked off into the estate. He kept looking back, waiting for the van to drive off. As he passed one of the blocks, he caught sight of what looked like a blurry old Davey with his hood up, shuffling and limping about by the bins in the basement. You didn't usually get them this far out of town, and he wondered if perhaps he was just living here, on the estate. He crossed the grass and a couple of loud boys playing a game of football went quiet while they eyed him up and Bully didn't waste any more time getting back to his own flat.

He was ready for a mouthful when he opened the door but it was nice and quiet for a change because everyone was still out. Phil had left Jack shut in the kitchen and when Bully opened the door, she hopped round him, sniffing at his ankles for the old and new smells. He felt a strange shudder of relief go through him. It had felt weird today being on his own without her and he realized that he had missed her and he was glad she was there, waiting for him to return. He'd been thinking that he shouldn't have left her. The ideas in his head had been ganging up on him on the way back, saying that Phil *might* have got rid of her or done something worse while he was out.

But, no, here she was. All in one piece. And he didn't push her away like he'd been doing for the last few weeks but got down on his hands and knees. He looked at her. And she sat right down on her one back leg and looked up at him, her Monkey Dog tail swishing on the linoleum floor.

"I know," he said. "I know…"

Bully ran the tap to get a cold drink of water. He listened to it splashing the sides of the stainless-steel sink before he drank it straight from the tap. Then he went to Cortnie's bedroom and found some black pens. He went back to the lounge and took out some of the begging letters he'd hidden under the couch and flicked through them until he found one with almost a blank page.

He was going to do something that he had never done outside of school in his life. He was going to write a letter. Because Phil was *right*. Camelot had decided to pay up but they were holding on to the money for him and his sister, putting it *in trust* until they were eighteen. So he had his half of the money. He just didn't have it for close to *five years*. It would be sitting somewhere in a big, big bank, waiting for him until then. The thing was, he knew he could not wait in the flat that long. He didn't have it in him. Not all that time with Phil and *her* and *it*. Even if sometimes they did all go out.

But he didn't want Jo thinking he wasn't grateful about the *risotto*. And he knew she would be upset and even angry with him if he phoned her up and told her what he was going to do, so he was putting it in a letter. And it was better than telling her on the internet because if he posted the letter tomorrow it would take *days* to get there and he'd be gone by then, back to the streets. Sending a letter with bad news was like planting a bomb. You didn't want to be around when it blew up.

It took him a good five minutes or so to get the words

right because he had to cross quite a few wrong ones out. Finally he found an old used envelope and crossed out the flat's address on the front and put Jo's on the back. All he needed was a new stamp.

As he was finishing up, the letter box started flapping. He froze and put his finger to his lips to *shh* Jack. And she went like stone, just like the hound at the cemetery. He was thinking it was maybe a moneylender and he didn't want to have to go explaining Phil's debt was nothing to do with him and his half of the money. Not with the darkness outside, getting ready...

There was more *flap, flapping*... And then his old name slipping in through the letter box, following along after him, tracking him down.

"Bully..."

30

He woke to the day, as always, surrounded by rubbish. Black bin liners leaking from their ripped corners right next to where he was sleeping. Old stuff and clothes everywhere. And books, piled up and flapping open. He kind of liked it that way though, being surrounded by all this mess.

"Brad... Brad... Bradley..."

"What?"

"You know what... Come on... Breakfast..." Rosie shouting up the stairs and then going back down to the kitchen.

He didn't want to get up. He'd been to school *every* day this week. And it was Wednesday and he deserved a lie-in, didn't he?

Jack did a hop round at the end of the bed. She gave his toes a lick and settled back down. She was getting heavier and Bully was pretty sure it wasn't just the extra food. She did a dog sigh that was almost exactly the same as a human one except it was just a little bit sadder because there were no words to go with it.

"All right for you," he said. "I never get a day off in this place." He sighed himself and then his head started rolling about, the insides of it thinking of getting back to sleep but already, despite himself, caught up in the new day.

He looked over at the empty window, full of blue sky. He put his glasses on and his skateboard underneath it sharpened up. He was supposed to wear them all day but he usually just put them on when he wanted to look at something specific, like a face in the distance or a number plate.

Rosie and John had bought him the skateboard a couple of weeks ago. Rosie had said Alex could teach him some tricks when he came home from *uni*. He'd said no, because he didn't want to scratch it. He liked waking up and seeing it there, propped up in the corner of his room, the newness still shining through the plastic. And he looked at it now. It wasn't the one he'd have bought but he loved it because someone had bought it for him.

"I suppose you want feedin' and cleanin'..." He sighed again and this time he got up. He reached out for his striped green tie, still in a leftover noose from yesterday, and put it on. And now except for his shoes he was wearing his whole school uniform. It saved time in the mornings.

He walked slowly down the stairs so his socks didn't slip on the smooth wood. He didn't see why Rosie wouldn't get carpet. He would buy them some, proper thick stuff like you got in pubs, when his money turned up. He would be eighteen, Alex's age, by then. It was a time so far in the future that he could only think of it as a science-fiction film.

He went through into the kitchen. Rosie was skating around a little yellow lake of dog wee, trying to make toast.

Bully pretended he hadn't seen the dog wee, though he knew Rosie was waiting for him to clean it up because it was *his* dog. She stopped what she was doing when he came in to look at him. But it wasn't about the dog wee.

"You woke up in that uniform, didn't you?" He didn't know how she could tell, he was even tucked in and everything.

"No..." he lied reflexively, but then added: "Not all of it." And he pointed to the tie.

"Bradley," she said. "What are we going to do with you? Eh?" But she didn't say it like a real question because they'd taken him on.

It wasn't legal yet exactly. Phil didn't want him, didn't need him now. He'd been happy to see the back of him when he got back from Emma's mum's place to find Jo and her dad patiently waiting there, watching *Mighty Ships* on the TV with Bully.

But though he'd moved in that night, they still had to go through the *process*. And that would take a while longer. Everything took a while in this new world of his.

He'd thought it was going to be like a holiday, that first night when him and Jacky had come back in the van to this big, posh house with next to nothing. But it hadn't felt like that at all. The next day had felt a bit like being in prison. Every day the same thing: get up at the same time, go to school, eat your food at the table and don't wear your clothes to bed. The list was long. And knowing he had to be here for years and years, waiting to get what was his.

And that had really worked him up at first.

"Errgh," said Jo, coming into the kitchen with lipstick on and eating a KitKat. "You do know there's dog wee all over the floor?" They both looked at her because, yes, they did know.

"No shit," said Bully.

Rosie didn't tell him off because she knew he was trying to cut down on his swearing, like people did with smoking.

"I was only saying," Jo said. "I'm off now anyway."

"What about your breakfast?" said Rosie. And Jo just waved the KitKat. She was at college now and Bully wished she was still at his new school, on the other side of the hill.

He followed her to the front door, lolloping along after her like a greyhound because he was getting taller now. She turned back to look at him. "Brads? Are my lips smudged?" He shook his head. He had his suspicions that she had a boyfriend now in this college place.

"How does it feel to be rich and famous?" She said it like a joke sometimes when she left the house because he wasn't rich, not yet anyway.

"Yeah, great," he said.

"See you later, alligator," she said. She picked up her bag. It was leather and all worn out. And though he knew she liked it like that, he was still going to buy her a new one. When he got his money or maybe even before then if he wandered into a shop with a bunch of receipts and helped himself to one, or got a paper round and saved up.

He was in two minds about it.

He went back to the kitchen and mopped up the dog wee with kitchen roll.

He washed his hands before he poured his cereal out because Rosie was still there.

"You off in a minute?" she said.

"Yeah, yeah…"

"You're going to go, aren't you, today?"

"Yeah?" he said, doing his surprised voice, like why would he not go to school on a Wednesday? As if that was the weirdest thing in the world *not* to do.

"Bradley. You will go, won't you? Mrs Avery can walk Jacky later because you don't have time now… What?" she said because he was smiling out the corner of his mouth.

He had a feeling Jacky was getting heavier because she was pregnant. Because she'd been hanging out with Mrs Avery's poodle *a lot*. He wasn't sure how he felt about that because both Mrs Avery and her dog were proper *posh* and spoke like it too. He reminded himself, though, that poodles had originally been bred as hunting dogs.

Ten minutes later, Rosie left to go to work. When he heard the door go, he said, "Go get your lead! Go on, girl." He *just* about had time to walk Jacky himself if he went into tutor group late.

He ran up Swain's Lane to the little circle of shops at the top of the village. He let Jacky chase a pigeon on the green, watched the pigeon just walk off, like it wasn't bothered by this three-legged dog.

A woman in black was waving at him. He squinted and nodded back. A lot of them were getting to know him up here now; he was the boy with the three-legged dog. And reminded of that, he stood and waited for her do a wee.

While he waited for Jacky he put on his glasses to scope out the village and immediately clocked the black Peugeot circling the green very slowly. *You can never be too careful...* But it was all right, it was Mr Douglas the newsagent, delivering the late papers by hand. He knew the plates, knew *all* the plates around the village. And the last three letters of Mr Douglas's were OES, which were the initials of the *Old English Sheepdog Society*. (Mr Douglas had not realized his plates were personalized until Bully had pointed it out to him.) He would, he decided, get a paper round and earn the money for Jo's bag, just in case he got caught nicking it and they took it off him in the cells. And also because he knew that nicking it would make her sad.

"Oh, Jacky, Jesus... No! You're pissing all wrong!" he said because she was trying to cock her leg like she used to, in fact like she was a *boy* dog, because bitches were never supposed to do that. And it was the leg that wasn't there... He looked round but nobody had seen her go down.

"Come on. We got to get back. You're making me *late*."

When he got back the post was on the mat and he kicked it over with his foot, trying to see who the letters were from without picking them up or even touching them. So far he'd had nothing addressed to him here and he liked it that way.

Eventually word would get round where the half-a-millionaire boy was living now. Words were free and the price of a second-class stamp was less than 59 pence, and those letters would start arriving soon just three houses in from the corner of Swain's Lane.

But not today. Just bills by the look of the brown envelopes and he would pay those for John and Rosie when he got his money or maybe before then. All their bills for everything, for ever.

He decided he *was* going to go to school. For the morning at least, to sign in. He didn't want other letters turning up here saying he was bunking off. So he made sure Jacky had plenty of food and water and reminded himself that Mrs Avery was coming round in a couple of hours and she *knew* about dogs. He grabbed his blazer and shoved it in his bag, ready to put it on as he went into tutor late. He shut the door and walked away from the house and then turned round as if to check it was still there.

He looked up to his room, right at the top in the roof of the house, the little square of glass divided into four. It looked a *little* bit like a prison cell from where he was but it didn't feel like a prison any more. Not now. It just felt like somewhere he was living, this place with his new … friends. A big old question mark in his heart, he couldn't quite bring himself to use the *f* word yet.

He thought he heard Jacky barking from the kitchen then, and he took a step back, and another, and then thought about going back.

But he stopped in his tracks because he knew Jacky didn't act like a baby when he was gone. She knew he was going to come back. She was trained. It was what you did with dogs; you trained them to trust you.

And making up for lost time, Bully got a move on, cold without his blazer, jogging up the hill, because school was on the other side.

Enjoyed this book? Tweet us your thoughts:

#LotteryBoy @WalkerBooksUK @MichaelByrneEtc

ACKNOWLEDGEMENTS

There was once a primary school teacher (so the story goes) who every year somehow managed to get the children in her class to paint and draw the most beautiful pictures in the school. When she was asked what her secret was, she said that she took the pictures away from the children before they finished them. Well, I have to say my experience of writing this book for children has been the exact opposite of that.

So, thank you to Zoe King, my agent, for going out on a limb and doing a whole lot more with the book than I could have ever done without her. And thank you to my editors: Gill Evans, who kept telling me to go away and do it again (but better); Lucy Earley, who really made the book sing; and Emily Damesick, who gave it a such a lovely rough polish at the end.

My thanks also to my mother and father, who worked so hard to give me a life they never had. And finally to Andrew Williams, the happiest Welshman I know and my bestest friend in the whole wide world

Michael Byrne worked as an English teacher in a secondary school just a mile from Heathrow. He then moved to Winchester to work as an airport taxi driver. The irony is not lost on him.

Michael lives with his daughter, Eve, and their cat, Chloe. He is now a full-time writer; this is his first novel.

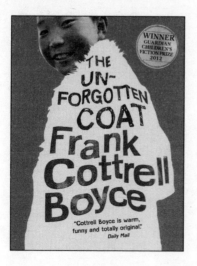

Carnegie Medallist Frank Cottrell Boyce transports readers from the steppe of Mongolia to the streets of Liverpool in a story that is compelling, miraculous and laugh-out-loud funny.

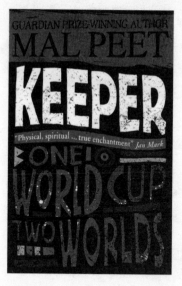

**WINNER OF THE
BRANFORD BOASE AWARD**

In a newspaper office, Paul Faustino, South America's top sports journalist, sits opposite the man they call El Gato – the Cat – the world's greatest goalkeeper. On the table between them stands the World Cup…

In the hours that follow, El Gato tells his incredible life story – how he, a poor logger's son, learns to become a World Cup-winning goalkeeper. And the most remarkable part of this story is the man who teaches him – the mysterious Keeper, who haunts a football pitch at the heart of the claustrophobic forest.

"Mal Peet [takes] the football novel into a new league."

The Guardian

"A remarkable and absorbing story with football at its heart, but superb storytelling in its soul."

Branford Boase Award panel

BOOK TALK (AND OTHER THINGS WE LOVE)

INTERVIEWS

PREVIEWS

COVER REVEALS

TRAILERS

WRITING TIPS

Scan the code to read
extracts from more books

For a chance to win other great reads visit

www.INK-SLINGERS.co.uk/win

Enjoyed this book? Tweet us your thoughts @WalkerBooksUK